The scream sound of a terrified woman—Scarlett.

Why had she stopped following him? Why had he let her?

"Scarlett?" He reversed course, staggering and tripping through the underbrush, cursing his bum leg. Cursing the men who'd caused it.

She screamed again, just as loudly but with a little less edge. His flashlight flickered on the path ahead of him as he charged back the way they'd come.

He plowed through the tree branches back onto the trail, which allowed him to move faster. "Scarlett?"

"I'm here, Jim."

His light picked her out, crumpled on the ground at his feet, and he jerked to a halt. He grabbed onto a tree branch to stop himself from falling on top of her.

"What happened?"

She pointed into the underbrush beside her. "Call 911."

ARMY RANGER REDEMPTION

—

CAROL ERICSON

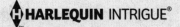

HARLEQUIN INTRIGUE®

For the water polo moms

Recycling programs
for this product may
not exist in your area.

ISBN-13: 978-0-373-74988-1

Army Ranger Redemption

Copyright © 2016 by Carol Ericson

Printed in U.S.A.

Carol Ericson is a bestselling, award-winning author of more than forty books. She has an eerie fascination for true-crime stories, a love of film noir and a weakness for reality TV, all of which fuel her imagination to create her own tales of murder, mayhem and mystery. To find out more about Carol and her current projects, please visit her website at www.carolericson.com, "where romance flirts with danger."

CAST OF CHARACTERS

Scarlett Easton—A local artist and native Quileute, she's a shaman in her tribe, but even these powers can't help her when she discovers a dead body on her property and a damaged army vet who has secrets to spare.

Jim Kennedy—An army ranger vet who has returned home to Timberline to deal with all the ghosts in his past, but that past collides with his future when he meets a beautiful artist who has her own ghosts to face.

Dax Kennedy—Jim's brother is an ex-con and a former member of the Lords of Chaos, a motorcycle gang that ruled the drug trade on the Washington Peninsula. Has he returned to Timberline to help his brother or drag him back into a life of crime?

Rusty Kelly—His death on Scarlett's property is the first sign that Timberline has not shrugged off its past association with drug trafficking.

Chewy Teller—A member of the Lords of Chaos, he returns to Timberline to take care of some old business.

Danny Easton—Scarlett's black-sheep uncle was in trouble with the law before; has he changed his ways or is he back to wreak more havoc?

Rocky Whitecotton—Expelled from the Quileute reservation for his criminal activity, his presence still casts a dark shadow over the residents of Timberline.

Evelyn Foster—Scarlett's grandmother may know more than she'll admit about the kidnappings from the past.

The Timberline Trio—Kayla Rush, Stevie Carson and Heather Brice were snatched from Timberline twenty-five years ago. The truth of their disappearance will rock Timberline.

Chapter One

Dread thumped against Scarlett's temples as she stepped out onto the porch of her cabin. Clouds rolled across the waxing crescent moon, teasing her as light and shadow played across the trees crowding up to her front door. Holding her breath, she hunched forward and squinted into the darkness until her eyes and muscles ached.

Since she couldn't see a thing beyond the tree line, she tilted her head and listened to the sounds of the forest—a rustle of dried leaves, the snap of a twig, the soft coo of a nighthawk.

Had her mind been playing tricks on her when, from inside the cabin, she'd heard the strangled cry? It could've been a wounded animal who'd moved on in his pain and suffering.

She hadn't been back in Washington one week from her art show in New York and already she was on edge. She no longer had to fear Jordan Young, the man who'd been harassing her. That

FBI agent, Duke Harper, had shot him dead to protect Beth St. Regis.

The Timberline Sheriff's Department had done a clean sweep of her property to make sure Young or his cohort hadn't planted any more traps. She had no reason to be afraid in her own cabin, on her own land. But she was.

Even before she'd heard what sounded like a muffled scream tonight, she'd been uneasy since her return to Timberline. She couldn't put her finger on the reason for the feeling, and had dismissed it as leftover angst from going into a dream state to help Beth sort out her own visions. Any time Scarlett used the extrasensory powers she'd inherited from her Quileute granny, it left her jumpy.

Cupping a hand around her mouth, she called out, "Hello? Anyone there?"

Not that she expected an answer, but it beat cowering on her porch. Only the wind responded as it whistled through the branches of the trees.

She huffed out a breath and backed up to her front door. She turned and glanced over her shoulder before stepping across the threshold and slamming the door behind her. The top dead bolt stuck as she tried to click it into place. After four tries, she gave up.

The dead bolt had been Granny's idea, but Scarlett hadn't used it in years. Now that she needed that extra layer of protection, the darned thing had rusted or jammed or whatever. She'd have to replace it.

She twitched the curtain back into place and returned to her chair in front of the fireplace, where a crackling blaze welcomed her. Five minutes later, with a book open in her lap and her legs curled beneath her, a loud knock on the front door disturbed the peace and set her heart racing again.

This time she went to the front door with a poker clutched in one hand and her cell phone in the other, even though she couldn't get cell reception out here. She jumped as a louder knock resounded through the room. Another thing this door was missing was a peephole. Why hadn't she gotten a peephole installed along with the dead bolt?

She shoved aside the curtain at the window next to the door and peered onto the porch. The light spilling onto the deck illuminated a large man. She swallowed and backed up, but the movement must've caught his eye and he pivoted toward the window.

"Are you okay in there?"

Sweeping aside the curtain, her cell phone prominently displayed, she asked, "Who are you? What do you want?"

"I'm Jim Kennedy. I have a place—" he waved behind him "—up the road. I heard a noise and came out to investigate. Was it you?"

Her muscles coiled. He sounded sincere, but it could all be a ploy to lure her outside and… "Jim Kennedy?"

"Yeah, my folks had this place before…before. The Butlers used to live here. Y-you're not Gracie Butler, are you?"

Kennedy. She knew the name. She'd known the man, or at least the boy—a rough boy, a solitary boy. "The Butlers sold out and moved to Idaho, where Gracie and her husband settled."

"So you're a local?"

They couldn't stand there yelling through the door all night. As she yanked it open, she had the fleeting thought that she'd known Wyatt Carson, too, and he'd turned out to be a psychopath.

The man before her stepped back, his eyes widening as if surprised she'd opened the door. Her gaze raked over his six-foot-something frame. He'd have nothing to fear from wandering around the forest at night.

"I'm Scarlett Easton." She thrust out her hand. "I grew up on the rez, but went to Timberline High. You were in my geometry class."

He blinked and heat rushed to her cheeks. Why in the world had she brought that up? She only remembered because she used to copy off his paper sometimes—not because she'd been intrigued by the loner who had a shock of black hair always falling in his eyes and rode a motorcycle.

She cleared her throat. "Mr. Stivers? Sophomore year?"

"Scarlett, yeah. You used to copy my answers all the time."

Her lips twisted into a smile. "Once in a while. Do you want to come in? I heard a noise, too. A scream, or…something."

"Sure."

She widened the door and stepped to the side as he limped over the threshold. She averted her gaze. The limp was new unless he'd just injured himself.

"Did you see anything out there?" The wind gusted as she shut the door, snatching it from her hand and slamming it.

Jim took a turn around the room with his halting gait, running his fingers along a table carved from a log, brushing his knuckles across a hand-painted pillow and studying the watercolor landscapes on the wall. "It's like a museum in here."

"Some of the pieces are for sale if you're interested."

Snapping his fingers, he said, "You were into all those art classes at school. You got suspended for painting a Native American mural on the wall outside the gym."

"Some of my best work."

He leaned forward to study a small painting of a storm-swept Washington coast. "Did you go outside right after you heard the noise?"

"I didn't say I went outside." She swallowed and took a step back to the door, curling her fingers around the knob.

"I heard a door slam." He straightened up and shoved his hands in the pockets of his black jeans. "I figured it had to be the door to this cabin since there aren't many others around here, are there?"

"N-no." Did he have to remind her about the isolation of their cabins? And how had he heard her door from a mile away? Since she'd bought this place, the Kennedy cabin had stood empty, but she knew it was a good distance away. She ran her tongue along her lower lip. "Let me get this straight. You heard a scream from inside your cabin, went outside to investigate and then heard my front door slam?"

"No." He moved in front of the fireplace, and a log rolled off the grate, causing a shower of sparks. "Do you have a poker?"

She reached behind her for the weapon she'd brought to the door for protection and grabbed it. If Jim Kennedy tried anything funny, she had no problem using the business end of this poker on him.

What *was* the business end of a poker?

He narrowed his dark eyes and they glittered behind half-mast lids. "I was already outside taking a walk when I heard the noise. I took off in the general direction of it, didn't hear anything else until the sound of a door shutting. I knew the Butler cabin was out this way, so I came over to investigate."

Rolling her shoulders, she strode forward with the poker in front of her and handed it to him— point first.

He took it around the middle and then prodded the log back into place, where it lit up in a quick blaze. "So, did you go outside after you heard the scream or just open your front door?"

"I stepped outside, but I didn't hear anything else, either. I'm thinking it might've been a wounded animal, and either it died or took off."

"Maybe. It sounded—" he shrugged "—familiar."

She thought he was going to say *human*, because that's what it sounded like to her.

"It gave me the chills." She held her hands out to the warmth of the fire, and the flickering flames caught the light from the many rings she wore on her fingers, creating a light show on the wall.

"I'll let you get back to your book." He tipped his chin at the book she'd left open on the recliner. "When I saw the lights on, I just wanted to make sure you were okay in here."

"Thanks." She led him to the front door and opened it wide for him to pass through. As he crossed the threshold, she inhaled his woodsy, masculine scent. On impulse, she touched his arm.

"Where've you been all these years, Jim Kennedy?"

He turned, brushing a lock of black hair from his face, and for the first time she noticed a scar across his forehead.

"Here and there."

She stood at the door watching him as he walked down the two steps with his halting gait. Just as she was about to close the door, a howl rose from the forest, causing a ripple of fear to skim across her flesh.

"It sounds closer here." Jim took off with surprising speed, and Scarlett followed him.

"Wait for me." She grabbed on to his leather jacket, stumbling against his broad back.

"Hey, who's out here?" Jim crashed through the branches of the trees as he illuminated the ground in front of him with a flashlight he'd pulled from his pocket.

He'd obviously come prepared, and then she saw the gun in his other hand. Prepared for what? She released her hold on him, and he continued forward, thrashing his way through the foliage, off the designated trail.

She staggered backward, twisting her fingers in front of her. What was Jim really doing out here and why did he have a gun? She knew hunting weapons, and that gun wasn't intended for use against some hapless deer.

As Jim called out again, she found her footing on the cleared path. She should make her way to the cabin and lock herself inside. This time she wouldn't open the door for anyone—former high school classmate or not. Jim Kennedy could take his sexy self back to here and there.

Tapping the light for her cell phone, she pivoted on the toes of her sneakers and took a step forward.

Then a hand grabbed her ankle.

Chapter Two

The scream chilled his blood. It was the sound of a terrified woman—Scarlett.

Why had she stopped following him? Why had he let her?

"Scarlett?" He reversed course, staggering and tripping through the underbrush, cursing his bum leg. Cursing the men who'd caused it.

She screamed again, just as loudly but with a little less edge. His flashlight flickered on the path ahead of him as he charged back the way they'd come.

He plowed through the tree branches back onto the trail, which allowed him to move faster. "Scarlett?"

"I'm here, Jim."

His light picked her out, crumpled on the ground at his feet, and he jerked to a halt. He grabbed on to a tree branch to stop himself from falling on top of her.

"What happened?"

She pointed into the underbrush beside her. "There. It's a man. H-he's injured or…"

Jim crouched beside her and aimed his flashlight at the bushes, where it illuminated an outstretched arm, hand fisted into the dirt.

He pushed aside the foliage that covered the man and reached out with two fingers to feel the pulse at his throat.

"He's dead. How did you even see him there without a light?"

She gasped, covering her mouth. "He grabbed my ankle. Are you sure he's dead?"

"What?" He scooped aside more of the underbrush and flattened his palm against the man's chest. Blood seeped through his shirt, moistening Jim's hand with its stickiness. He bent forward, putting his ear close to the man's nose and mouth.

"Call 911."

"I can't get reception out here. I'll have to at least walk down the access road to the front."

He gestured to the man's body. "He's dead. He's not going anywhere. I'll come with you."

"What happened to him?" She clambered to her knees, and he held out the hand that didn't have blood on it.

"He has a chest wound. I can't tell what did it, but he lost a lot of blood. I'm surprised he had the strength to reach out and grab you, or even the wherewithal to realize anyone was passing."

She grabbed his hand, and he pulled her up beside him, where he could smell her musky-sweet scent.

"He must've been the one moaning out here. Maybe he lost consciousness and then came to when we passed him. He reached out to me as a last-ditch effort." She bent her leg at the knee and rubbed her ankle.

"Let's go." He tugged on her hand to get her away from the dead guy in the bushes. "From the looks of the blood pumping out of his chest, he was fast on his way out and wouldn't have survived even if we had discovered him when he was moaning."

As they burst onto the access road, he aimed his light at the ground and hurried across the gravel and dirt, practically dragging Scarlett behind him as she kept trying her phone.

He didn't want to run into whatever…or whoever that man had encountered.

When they reached Scarlett's mailbox on the road, she nudged his arm. "Got it."

"Let me report it." He took the phone from her and spoke to the emergency operator, giving her what he could. When he finished the call, he dropped the phone back into Scarlett's palm.

She asked, "Did you see his face? Do you know him?"

"I didn't get a good look at his face, but I doubt I know him. It's been a while since I've been back to Timberline." He held out his hand in front of him and lit it up with the beam from his flashlight. "I got his blood on my hand, though."

"Ugh. Do you want me to get a towel while we wait for the cops? I have paper towels in my car."

"I'll leave it until the sheriff's department can have a look at it." He jerked his thumb over his shoulder. "What happened back there? Why'd you stop following me?"

"I—" Her eyes darted to his pocket where he'd stashed his weapon. "I didn't want to go any deeper in the forest."

Especially in the company of a man with a gun—a man she'd just met even though they'd been high school classmates years ago. Smart girl.

"And then the guy just grabbed your ankle? Hard?"

"Not that hard but enough to surprise me and trip me up."

"When did you realize he was hurt?"

"I kicked out when I fell, to loosen his hold. I'd already had my cell phone out for the light. When I was on the ground, the little beam of light illuminated his hand, and I could see that it was limp. His arm wasn't moving, but I screamed again just in case."

"I heard you, loud and clear—both times. You didn't see his face?"

"I wanted to run the hell out of there, but I couldn't move. My muscles froze. I certainly didn't want to look at him. Did you see his face?"

"Nope." He shook his head. "Maybe you know him. Maybe he was a friend on his way to visit you."

"Me?" Her dark brows shot up. "I don't think so. The only people who come out here to visit me are my cousins, Jason and Annie. And that wasn't Jason's hand."

"We'll find out who he is soon enough." He held up one finger. "Sirens."

The revolving lights on top of the emergency vehicles cast an eerie glow in the misty air as they flew down the small road to Scarlett's cabin.

Jim waved the flashlight in the air to flag them down.

The vehicles—one ambulance, one fire truck and a squad car—squealed to a stop in front of Scarlett's mailbox.

Jogging next to the squad car, Jim knocked on the passenger window, and the deputy buzzed it down. "You can go up the access road. The body's in the woods, just off the trail."

The deputy gestured out his window for the ambulance to make the turn onto the access road, and then he followed it.

Jim and Scarlett caught up just as the officer

was getting out of his cruiser. "What's going on, Scarlett? More shots fired out here? More bear traps?"

Jim shifted his gaze to Scarlett's face. She hadn't told him about any shots being fired out here or any bear traps. That's all he needed for his other leg—a bear trap.

"Cody, you remember Jim Kennedy, don't you?" She swept her arm in his direction.

With his left hand, Jim shook Cody Unger's hand. Must be Deputy Cody Unger now. He'd been the high school quarterback and an all-around good guy. Jim hadn't known him well—different circles.

"Kennedy." Unger nodded. "Did you find him?"

"Scarlett did." Jim held up his right palm. "But I checked him out. He has a wound to the chest and lost a lot of blood. This way."

As Jim led the way with his flashlight, Scarlett asked Unger, "Where's Sheriff Musgrove?"

"I called him. He's not feeling well, told me to handle it."

Jim stopped and pointed to the arm flung out on the trail. "That's him. The rest of his body is beneath those bushes. I don't know how he got there, but both Scarlett and I heard a scream or a cry earlier. Must've been him."

"I have a couple of other deputies en route. They can canvass this area." Unger squatted down next to the body and pushed the bushes away from it while shining his flashlight on the man's face. "Doesn't look familiar. Let's get out of the way and let the EMTs do their thing."

The EMTs squeezed past them as Jim and Scarlett followed Unger back to the access road.

"Do you mind if we talk inside your cabin, Scarlett?"

"I was hoping you'd ask." She sniffled. "It's cold out here."

They ran into the other two deputies in front of Scarlett's cabin and Unger instructed them to look for evidence in the area and to check for the man's ID.

Once inside the cabin, Unger pulled a kit out of the black bag slung across his body. "I'm going to scrape some of that blood from your hand and get it on a slide. Then you can wash it off."

Jim held out his hand, palm up, and Unger ran a stick over his skin to collect a sampling of the blood. He transferred it to a slide, sealed another slide on top of the first one and dropped it into a plastic bag. "You can clean up now. Thanks for preserving the evidence."

Scarlett tapped his arm. "Bathroom's the first door on your right."

The art gallery spilled over to the bathroom with a border of flowers and cupids painted on the wallpaper and a mirror that looked fit for a wood sprite, with carved leaves and flowers curling around its edges.

Jim soaped up his hand and removed the blood. He didn't want to mess up any of Scarlett's artfully placed towels with residual blood, so he plucked a couple of tissues from the box and wiped off his hands just in case. He dropped them in the toilet and flushed.

He hunched forward, studying his reflection in the mirror, and grimaced. How the hell had he gotten mixed up with a dead body his first week back in Timberline? Not exactly the way to keep a low profile.

When he returned to the front room, he interrupted Scarlett reenacting the moment when the man grabbed her ankle.

"So, I kicked out, fell on the ground and screamed, just not sure of the order of those actions."

Unger turned to him, his notebook in hand. "That's when you returned? When you heard Scarlett scream?"

"I ran back, she pointed out the body and I felt his pulse and his chest." He wiped his damp hand on his jeans. "That's how I got his blood on me. I felt for a pulse first and listened for his breath, too. He was dead."

"You ever had any CPR training, Kennedy?" Unger tapped his pencil against his pad.

"Six years as an army ranger sniper. I know

the signs of a dead body when I see 'em, and I know when it's too late to render aid."

As he held Unger's gaze, he heard Scarlett's sharp intake of breath.

A slow smile spread across Unger's face. "I guess you know what you're doing. Did either of you recognize him?"

"I didn't get a good look at his face and Scarlett didn't see his face at all. He had a beard. I felt that when I listened for his breath."

Scarlett asked, "Did you recognize him, Cody? You looked at his face, didn't you?"

"Older guy, beard, long, reddish hair. I haven't seen him around, but the conditions out in the woods are not optimal for identifying a body." He shoved his notebook in his pocket. "I got your stories. If I have any other questions, I'll let you know. It could just be an accident. I don't know yet what caused his wound, but if it turns out to be homicide, we'll call in the boys from county and they might have additional questions for you."

Jim followed Unger to the front door and stepped out onto the porch with him. Scarlett tagged along, slinging her jacket over her shoulders. Did she plan to go out again?

Unger pointed to the trees crowding close to Scarlett's cabin. "You should get those removed, Scarlett. Most cabins out here have some sort of clearing around them. I don't know why the Butlers never did it when they had the place."

"It's one of the features that drew me to the cabin—the privacy. I need it for my work."

Jim crossed his arms. "Don't artists need natural light?"

"Not for the kind of work I do."

He knew nothing about art or artists, except the kind that did tattoos, so he'd keep his mouth shut.

Scarlett gasped and grabbed his arm. "They're bringing him out."

Peering through the trees that ringed Scarlett's property, Jim could make out the EMTs wheeling a gurney from the woods onto the access road.

They all made their way down the path, through the trees, and stopped short of the gurney at the mouth of the ambulance doors. The EMTs had yanked the white sheet over the dead man's face.

One of the guys turned to Unger. "Looks like he succumbed to a stab wound to the chest— multiple stab wounds."

Scarlett swayed beside him, and Jim put a steadying arm around her shoulders. "Did it happen here, on Scarlett's property?"

The EMT shrugged. "I can't tell. That's for those deputies thrashing around out there to figure out."

Unger whistled. "I'll call Sheriff Musgrove right away. We're going to need county out here now."

"Should we wait for the county coroner?"

"Take him to the morgue at the hospital. The county coroner can work there."

Unger turned to go back into the woods and Jim held up his hand to stop him. "Is Scarlett safe here? The guy could've been murdered twenty-five yards from her front door."

Scarlett's body stiffened beside him and he drew her closer.

"I'm calling the county sheriff's department right now. They'll probably be here the rest of the night. I don't think Scarlett has anything to worry about." Unger charged off toward the crime scene.

As the EMTs adjusted the straps on the body, Scarlett said, "Wait. C-can we see his face? I just want to make sure it's not anyone I know, although if Cody didn't recognize him I doubt I will."

"Sure." The EMT whipped back the sheet from the man's face.

Jim clenched his jaw as sour bile rose from his gut. Scarlett and Unger might not know the murdered man, but Jim did.

And if the man hadn't already been dead, he might've killed him himself.

Chapter Three

Scarlett swallowed as she studied the dead man's face, half obscured by his bushy beard and mustache, some sort of tattoo creeping up his neck with an *L* and a *C* intertwined. She'd never been a portraitist, but if she had been she'd want this guy's likeness on canvas. Even in death, he wore his life story on his face, etched in every line and wrinkle.

She blew out a breath. "I don't know him. Jim?"

"Never saw him before in my life."

The EMT tugged the sheet back over the man's face and loaded him into the ambulance.

Unger returned with his deputies. "The county sheriff's department should be out here shortly, Scarlett. They don't need to disturb you tonight, but the lead detective will probably want to talk to both of you tomorrow. Going anywhere, Kennedy?"

"I'm staying at my…my place."

Scarlett glanced at him out of the corner of her eye. The Kennedy cabin had been the closest residence to hers, but nobody had lived there since she'd bought the Butler place. Apparently, Jim Kennedy, the town enigma, had been off to war with the army rangers all these years.

When the EMT had lifted the covers on the dead man, Jim had moved away from her. She hadn't minded his arm draped over her shoulders or the solid presence of his muscular frame, although she'd never been one to lean on a man. Her own father had died in a car accident along with her mother, and her uncle had been a black sheep, ostracized from the reservation.

She scooped her hair back from her face. "I'm going to call it a night. Tell those county deputies they can talk to me anytime they want, but mornings are best, before I get to work."

Unger smacked the side of the ambulance as its engine started. "I'm going to back out and let these guys out of here, but I'm sticking around to wait for the county guys."

"Okay if I leave, Unger?" Jim shoved his hands into his pockets where he must've still had his weapon stashed.

If the man had been shot instead of stabbed, would Jim have told Unger about his gun? If he had a gun, maybe he had a knife.

Scarlett closed her eyes and dragged in a deep breath. Nothing about Jim screamed cold-blooded killer, but she couldn't shake the co-incidence of his appearance followed by the discovery of a dead body on her property.

"You can leave. Again, just be available in case anyone wants to ask you any more questions."

Scarlett pivoted on the gravel. "Hope you can figure out what happened to that poor man."

Jim drew up beside her with his flashlight. "I'll walk you back to your place, if that's okay."

"If you want, but I think I'll be fine with half the Timberline Sheriff's Department on my property and the county sheriffs showing up in a few."

"I can take a look around and check your doors and windows—for when all those deputies leave."

A little chill zapped the back of her neck, and she hunched her shoulders. "That's a creepy thought."

"Not my intention to scare you, but sometimes a little fear is a good thing."

They returned to her cabin and Jim flicked the broken dead bolt. "You can start here by getting this replaced, and you might want a peephole in the door so you don't have to look out that window."

"Funny enough, I noticed those deficiencies myself when you banged on my door."

"Why don't you give me a tour?"

She spread her arms. "This is the great room, perfect for entertaining three guests at one time."

His lips twisted as he checked the front window. Then he moved to the other two. "At least they all have working locks."

"At least?"

"Anyone can smash a window."

"Thanks for that."

"But then you'd wake up and the intruder would lose his advantage, and you could always come at him with this." He strolled to the fireplace and replaced the poker she'd snatched for her defense when he'd first come to her place. "Do you have a gun?"

"A gun? I hate guns."

He pulled his own gun from his pocket and caressed the handle. "You hate guns because you're afraid of them. If you learned how to take care of a gun and all the safety measures associated with gun ownership, you might feel differently."

Shaking her head, she gritted her teeth. "I doubt it. Almost everyone around here has at least a shotgun and spends a lot of their time hunting defenseless animals."

"I agree. You don't have anything to fear from a wild animal." He returned his gun to his pocket. "I spent my time in the army hunting a different kind of animal—definitely not defenseless."

"You used to hunt, though, didn't you?" She

snapped her fingers. "That's why you became a sniper. You were a great shot."

"Something like that." He pointed toward the kitchen. "Do you have a back door?"

"Two of them—a side door off the kitchen and then a back door from the addition. That's another thing I liked about this cabin. The Butlers had added a room to the back of the house, which made a perfect studio."

He checked the kitchen door and tapped the wood. "You need a dead bolt on this door, too."

"I'll get someone out to do both doors, same key."

He stood in the middle of her kitchen, dwarfing it. He'd even been buff as a teenager. Instead of playing team sports for the high school, Jim had spent his time working out and lifting weights.

From the way his shoulders filled out his jacket, he hadn't given up the weights.

"You know what you need in this kitchen?"

"Besides a twenty-four-hour chef?"

"A landline telephone. You can't keep running to the end of the road in an emergency."

She hunched over the kitchen counter, planting her elbows on the tile. "I came back here, bought this cabin to get away from it all, to work, not to get all plugged in."

"After what just happened out there—" he

jerked his thumb over his shoulder "—you need to think about your safety."

She widened her eyes. "Why? Do you think there's a serial killer on the loose or something? I'm not happy that someone died outside my cabin, but I don't think it has anything to do with me. From the looks of the guy, it could've been a bar fight or drug related."

Jim straightened up so fast from where he'd been bent over looking for a phone jack, he almost hit his head on the bottom of the cabinet.

"Why would you say that?"

"I don't know. He looked a little rough around the edges, could've been using."

"The point is, we don't know his story." He limped from the kitchen and tipped his chin toward the short hallway. "Okay if I take a look in the other rooms?"

"There are just the two bedrooms. You already visited the one bathroom, and then the room at the end of the hall—my studio."

He pushed into the bathroom and placed his palms flat against the small, beveled-glass window. "Someone can slide this up and out. You can buy a rod to put across the top of the slider to prevent that, or you can even use a pencil."

"Good idea. I never realized how unsafe I was before."

"You never found a dead body on your property before—have you?"

"That was a first, although I guess it's not all that rare for Timberline cabins to be housing dead bodies. Did you hear about Jordan Young killing his mistress twenty-five years ago and stuffing her body in the chimney of his cabin?" She sucked in a breath between her teeth and shivered.

"I read about the whole thing online when I got here. So much for peaceful little Timberline."

He checked the windows in the guest bedroom, and then she led him to her own room. As he took a turn around the bedroom, she actually blushed—not out of modesty but because she'd just had a sudden vision of this man spread out on her bed.

"You should keep these closed at night." He yanked the curtains together and she jumped. "Are you still nervous?"

"It's not every day someone is murdered in your neighborhood." She caught her lower lip between her teeth. She should be feeling more anxious about that instead of daydreaming about Jim Kennedy in all his naked glory. She'd put it down to shock.

He tilted his head and that lock of dark hair fell over one eye—just like in high school. "Let's take a look at that back door."

As she led him to her studio, she clasped her hands in front of her, twirling her ring around her middle finger. She usually didn't invite people into her inner sanctum, unless they were other artists. Not even potential clients saw her workspace.

Dragging in a breath, she threw open the door and flicked on the light.

Jim froze at the doorway, his mouth hanging slightly ajar. "I've never seen anything like this before in my life."

"Well—" she waved her arms around "—it's an artist's studio."

"You're very…productive." He swiveled his head from side to side, taking in the work on the walls, canvases stacked in the corner and unfinished pieces languishing on easels stationed around the room. "And kind of schizophrenic."

"I guess that's one way of putting it."

"You've got normal stuff over here—" he flung out his right arm "—and…different kind of stuff over here."

"Landscape watercolors on the right and modern, abstract oils on the left."

"Let me guess." He pointed to a painting comprising of skyscrapers, a pair of eyes and a wolf head. "This is the expensive stuff."

"Good guess." She held her breath waiting for him to ask her to explain the painting.

He studied it for several seconds with his head

to one side and then shrugged. "This room isn't secure at all."

She released the breath. "Because of the glass wall."

"It must look incredible during the day, but at night anybody could peer right into this room. If you keep expensive work in here, I'd think you'd want to protect it better."

"This is Timberline. I really didn't expect to move back here and experience a crime wave." She rapped on the glass. "What do you suggest?"

"This is the back door?" He navigated through the easels and stands and yanked on the handle of the sliding glass door. He crouched down and inspected the track. "You can put a rod in here for an extra measure of safety in case someone breaks the lock. A camera wouldn't be a bad idea, either."

Twisting her braid around her hand, she sighed. "I might as well go back to the big city."

"That man who died tonight probably has nothing to do with you."

"Don't try to make me feel better now after you just did a security check on my home…and found it woefully inadequate."

"Problem is, we don't know what he was doing out there, why he was killed or who killed him."

He straightened up, grasping the door handle for support. She would've offered a hand, but Jim didn't seem like the type of man who would accept assistance easily.

"Hopefully the county sheriff's department can figure that out. I don't need any more people lurking around my cabin, causing trouble."

"Jordan Young was after that TV reporter, not you, right?"

"Jordan turned out to be Beth St. Regis's biological father. He'd murdered her mother, his mistress, twenty-five years ago and sold Beth on the black market when she was a baby. He just turned his attentions toward me because I was helping Beth." She shivered and pressed her hands against her stomach. "Pure evil."

"He figured if anyone noticed his daughter's disappearance, he could pass it off as another Timberline kidnapping?"

"Something like that, but nobody noticed the disappearance of mother and daughter since Beth's mother had moved away after the pregnancy and had just returned to Timberline. Young had kept them hidden away in his cabin until he killed Angie, Beth's mother."

"Makes you wonder." He shoved one hand in his pocket and stared out the wall of windows at the forest lurking in the darkness beyond.

"Wonder what?"

"If there was an active black market for children, maybe that's what happened to the Timberline Trio."

"Not you, too." She shut off the light in the studio. "Ever since Wyatt Carson kidnapped those three children to recreate the Timberline Trio so he could play the hero, everyone and his brother have been snooping around looking into the Timberline Trio case."

"You think that's a bad idea?" He'd turned from the window and his eyes glimmered in the dark room.

"It's over." She'd never admit to him that she had her own reasons for finding out what had happened twenty-five years ago. She'd never admit that to anyone, since curiosity about the case seemed to put a target on your back.

He said, "I suppose it's never over for the families. Look what it did to Wyatt Carson. Losing his younger brother like that must've jarred something loose in his psyche for him to go on and kidnap those children years later."

"You're right." She stepped back into the light from the hallway. "I don't mean to be insensitive, but…"

"You're Quileute."

"What's that supposed to mean?" She jutted out her chin.

"Just that I know your people had some fears and superstitions around the whole Timberline

Trio case." He held up his hands. "Hey, they weren't the only ones."

As far as she could recall, Jim never had a problem with the Quileute, but his father was another story—loudmouthed bigot. Members of her tribe had been in a few barroom brawls with Slick Kennedy.

He'd gotten the nickname Slick because of his movie-star handsomeness and pumped-up physique. Her gaze tracked over Jim as he stood in the middle of the room, and she swallowed. The apple hadn't fallen too far from *that* tree.

But Jim had never been in any trouble with her people, although all the guys her age had been wary of him because of his father, his brother and his father's buddies—beer-drinking, bigoted bikers.

She lifted and dropped her shoulders quickly. "Yeah, there were some crazy stories going around at the time."

He crossed the room and joined her at the door. "Anyway, you might want to look into securing this place better—at least until the deputies can figure out why that man dropped dead in the woods outside your cabin."

"I'll do that, thanks." She closed the door to the studio. Halfway down the hallway, she turned suddenly and Jim bumped into her. She placed a palm against his chest where his heart thundered beneath her touch. "Sorry."

His body tensed as he stepped away from her, and she dropped her hand.

"What are you doing back here, Jim?"

His lids lowered over his eyes and he studied her from beneath his thick, dark lashes. "Trying to get away from it all, just like you."

She blinked and turned, calling over her shoulder. "How long have you been out of the army?"

"Over a year."

"Is that…is that what happened to your leg?"

"Long story."

It didn't sound like he had any intention of sharing it with her. Maybe he'd loosen up after a few beers or a shot of whiskey.

When they reached the living room, he made a beeline for the front door. "See you around."

Scarlett blinked. "I was going to offer you something for your trouble tonight and for staying with me. Beer? Coffee?"

"I'm good, thanks."

Now it seemed as if he couldn't get away from her fast enough. Must've thought she was prying into his business. She followed him to the front door, which he'd already opened.

He stepped out onto the dark porch.

"Oops, I turned off my porch light. Be careful. I have some plants…"

As he turned, Jim tripped over one of the pots and stumbled down the two steps, falling to the ground.

He cursed on his way down and landed with a thud in the dirt.

"I'm so sorry." Scarlett switched on the porch light and flew down the steps. As she lowered herself to the bottom step to help Jim, his bare back, exposed by his shirt hiking up, drew her gaze.

Shock tingled through her body as she saw the edge of Jim's tattoo—an *L* and a *C* curled together—just like the tattoo on the dead man.

Chapter Four

"Dammit." If Scarlett touched him or tried to help him, his humiliation would be complete.

She jerked back and pushed to her feet. She must've sensed the vibe coming off him.

"Why'd you turn off the porch light?" He rolled to his back and peered up at her wide eyes. "I'd forgotten those damned potted plants were there."

"Yeah, sorry. It's a habit for me to turn off that light when I come inside for the night." She took another step up, reaching for the door behind her. "You okay?"

"I'm all right." He hoisted up to his feet and brushed the dirt from his jeans.

"Maybe one of the deputies can give you a ride home."

She wasn't offering? He didn't blame her, the way he'd snapped at her. Wasn't her fault he had a gimp leg.

"I think I can make it." He stomped his boots on the ground. "No permanent damage, or at least no *more* permanent damage."

"Okay, then. Good night." She slipped into her cabin and slammed the door.

That spark he'd felt between them had just been extinguished. The fall made her realize he was damaged goods. A woman like that needed a strong man to match her, not some physically weakened, brain-addled vet.

He trudged through the trees toward the deputies canvassing the crime scene, giving them a wide berth to avoid being questioned tonight. He couldn't handle it right now.

Seeing Rusty Kelly's dead body had been a shock. What was Rusty doing back here? That type always rode in packs. Did that mean the rest of them were close on his heels? Was it a coincidence that Rusty had turned up dead a week after Jim had arrived in Timberline?

He edged around the squad cars and took the long way back to his cabin by following the road. When he got back to his place, he withdrew his Glock and checked out the perimeter of the cabin.

Unlike Scarlett's place, this cabin had a wide clearing around it that extended all the way to the road. He believed in having an unobstructed view of whatever was coming at him.

But he hadn't seen Scarlett Easton coming at

him. He'd noticed the smoke from her chimney since he'd been back, but he'd figured it was Gracie Butler living in her folks' place. He hadn't been prepared for a dark-haired beauty to hit him like a thunderbolt.

Scarlett had been something of a mystery in high school—a rebel but not a bad girl, lost both of her folks in a car accident. She'd never partied much unless it was on the rez, and she'd traveled with a pack of very protective guys from her tribe. That bunch wouldn't have let him within two feet of Scarlett, but then they'd judged him based on his old man. He didn't blame them.

Satisfied there were no strangers or, worse, people he knew lurking around the cabin, he went inside. He locked the door behind him and faced the room, his breath coming in short spurts.

Squeezing his eyes shut, he massaged his bad leg. It didn't hurt him anymore, but sometimes it ached in remembrance.

He dragged in a deep breath, but it didn't do any good. Even with his eyes closed, he could feel the room spinning, the darkness closing in on him.

He managed to make it to the couch, dragging his left leg behind him. Collapsing to the cushions, he ripped off his jacket and dropped it to the floor. He sank, his head in his hands, his fingers digging into his scalp.

The heat. He couldn't take the heat. He yanked off his shirt and the T-shirt beneath it. He bunched them both into a ball and pressed it against his face to mop the sweat pouring from his brow.

Falling to his side on the couch, he let out a low moan. Then the images began flashing behind his closed lids. He drove his fists against his eyeballs to make the pictures in his head go away...but they kept coming.

He needed his medication. How had he thought he could do without it, especially in this place?

He needed a drink. He needed to sleep. He needed a warm body.

He needed Scarlett Easton.

"HE WAS KILLED somewhere else?" Scarlett cupped her hands around her mug of tea and inhaled the fragrant steam as it rose to meet the cool morning air. "I suppose that's...a relief."

Deputy Collins, from the county's homicide division, nodded. "We're thinking maybe someone stabbed him in a car or even before, and then loaded him up and dumped him out on the side of the road. There were some blood spots on the asphalt. Then he dragged himself through the woods. Maybe he was heading toward your cabin to get help."

She shivered. "He didn't have a cell phone on him?"

"No, and he didn't have a wallet."

"You haven't identified him yet?" She laced her fingers around her cup.

"Not yet. The coroner's doing an autopsy this morning, and we'll get his prints and DNA. Nobody's reporting anything yet—no missing persons, no accidents, no barroom fights."

She didn't know why she wasn't telling this nice deputy all about the tattoo the dead man shared with Jim Kennedy. Why hadn't Jim said something? Maybe he hadn't seen the man's tattoo emblazoned on his neck. But why did he have the same one?

How could that possibly be a coincidence? It had an *L* and a *C*. It's not like it was the tattoo of a hula girl. It meant something.

She kicked the toe of her boot against the planter on the corner of her porch, the same one Jim had tripped over in the dark.

What had happened to his leg?

The man was as full of secrets as the boy had been—and just as dangerous. She'd been as drawn to him last night as she'd been in high school, but this time she'd sensed an answering spark of interest.

She hadn't been alone in her feverish daydreams about Jim Kennedy during high school. Lots of the girls at school—even the popular ones—had whispered and giggled about Jim, but none of them, including her, would've been allowed to go out with him. He was every parent's nightmare—long hair, motorcycles and a bad, bad family.

It had just been Jim, his older brother and their father. They all rode motorcycles, and the older brother and Slick had been hard drinkers and hard partyers. She had no idea what had happened to his mother.

Deputy Collins glanced at his notepad. "A Mr. Kennedy was with you when you discovered the body?"

"That's right. He lives in the next cabin up the road."

"Thanks for your help, Ms. Easton. We'll contact you if there's anything else or if we think you might be in some kind of danger."

"Danger?" Her pulse jumped. "You mean if the man's death was some random murder and there's a killer on the loose?"

"I don't think that's the case. He looked like a rough customer, probably ran with a rough crowd. Once we ID him, we might be able to put your mind at ease. You probably don't have anything to worry about."

Yeah, except for her attraction to Jim Kennedy, who had the same tattoo as the dead man. That worried her.

"Well, I'll be here if you have any more information for me."

He tipped his hat, and the copse of trees ringing her property swallowed him up as he made his way to his car.

Through narrowed eyes, she watched him get into his car, the last of the emergency vehicles that had been out here all night.

If this *rough customer* had died in the woods beyond her cabin as a result of a fight, she had nothing to fear. She hadn't seen anything. She couldn't point the finger at his killer, and she didn't know the dead man.

But if someone was running around Timberline stabbing people and dumping them on her property, then she had plenty to fear.

She snorted and took a gulp of lukewarm tea. Why would someone want to do that? She knew nothing about anything—no more dream quests for her, no more psychic mumbo jumbo, as her cousin Jason called it.

Except that she did know something. She knew Jim Kennedy and the dead man shared the same tattoo, and Jim hadn't said a word about it to anybody.

She retreated to her cabin and slammed the door. She'd come back to Timberline to work, and she planned to keep her head down and do just that.

She didn't have the time or energy to sort out a brooding war vet with trouble in his eyes and sin on his lips.

"IS THIS FOR your granny, Scarlett, or have you taken up knitting, too?"

Scarlett dropped the two skeins of yarn on the counter. "Me? Knit? You've gotta be kidding."

Barbara, the owner of A Stitch in Time, rang up the yarn on her register. "You're so artistic, you could probably do it."

"Totally different kind of art, Barbara."

"I like those pretty landscapes you do." Barbara pursed her lips and stuffed the yarn into a bag.

Scarlett covered her smile with her hand. Barbara didn't have to like her modern art—enough people did.

"Thanks, Barbara."

"You know," Barbara said, and shook her finger at Scarlett, "you should do some local crafts, like Vanessa Love does with those Libby Love frogs. Maybe something… Native American."

"You mean like dream catchers and tom-toms?" Scarlett raised her brows. "Ah, no. I don't do that kind of stuff."

Reaching for her wallet, Scarlett glanced out the window just in time to see her cousin duck into Sutter's Restaurant. "How much do I owe you, Barbara? I just saw Jason go into Sutter's and I'm going to try to catch him."

"That'll be ten dollars and fifty cents. Your cousin is always at Sutter's." She cleared her throat. "Not that I'm spying out my window, mind you."

"He's dating a waitress there." Scarlett put a ten on the counter and dug in her purse for two quarters. "Thanks, Barbara. You're a lifesaver for finding that purple shade for me."

"Anything for your granny, Scarlett."

Scarlett tucked the bag beneath her arm and charged across the street to Sutter's. Jason had been shirking his duty in checking up on Granny when Scarlett had been out of town and she planned to read him the riot act. He couldn't dump all the responsibility on his sister, Annie.

The lunch crowd from Evergreen Software was thinning out, and Scarlett zeroed in on Jason lounging at the bar adjacent to the dining area. She waved off the hostess. "I'm going to the bar."

She swung around to the side of the restaurant and snuck up behind Jason, tapping him on the shoulder. She grinned as he almost fell off the bar stool.

"Wow, cuz, are you trying to give me a heart attack?"

She shook the yarn bag in his face. "It's gonna be worse than that if you don't start checking up on Granny more regularly."

"She doesn't want to see me. She'd rather see you and Annie."

"That's ridiculous and it doesn't matter. She's getting up there in age, and you need to check on her. You can't leave that up all up to Annie. She's busy with her new cleaning business."

He shrugged, whipping his long hair back from his face. "Heard you found a dead body outside your place last night."

"That's a neat way to change the subject." She perched on the stool next to him. "Yeah, some older guy—long, reddish-gray hair. I'd never seen him before."

"And I thought your problems were over when that FBI agent killed Jordan Young."

"Problems? The county sheriff's department thinks someone dumped him on the road near my place and he made his way into the woods." She folded her arms on the bar. "It's not my problem."

Chloe, Jason's girlfriend, approached them, tucking a notepad into her apron. "Did they find out who the dead guy is yet?"

Scarlett rolled her eyes. "Does everyone know?"

"Of course." Chloe snapped her gum. "It's Timberline."

Jason pinched Chloe's hip. "I gotta go. Just popped in to say hi and, yes, I'll check up on Granny more, Scarlett."

"I'll see you after work." Chloe's eyes widened as she stared past Jason's shoulder. "Who is that?"

Scarlett jerked her head around just in time to meet Jim's gaze across the dining room.

Jason growled. "He's that racist SOB biker."

Scarlett jabbed her cousin with her elbow. "Jim's not like that. You're talking about his father. What *did* happen to Slick Kennedy, anyway?"

"Someone killed him in Seattle a few years back...and nobody around here gave a damn." He kicked Scarlett's foot. "Shh. He's coming this way."

"Why's he coming over here?" A slow blush spread across Chloe's cheeks, and Jason gave his girlfriend a sharp look.

"H-he was with me last night when I found the body."

Jason transferred his look from Chloe to her.

"I guess he has his dad's place now. It's down the road from mine."

As Jason opened his mouth, Scarlett nudged the leg of his stool to shut him up.

"Are you okay? Did you get any sleep?" Jim studied her through dark-smudged eyes while running a hand through his messy hair.

"Looks like I got more than you." She wanted to ask him if he'd injured himself falling off her porch, but he wouldn't appreciate her concern—especially not in front of Jason and Chloe.

"I have a hard time sleeping in that place, dead body or no dead body."

She tipped her head toward Jason. "This is my

cousin, Jason Foster, and his girlfriend Chloe Rayman."

Jim took Chloe's hand and the girl looked ready to faint. Then he shook Jason's hand, despite the once-over her cousin was giving him. "You know anyone interested in some old Harleys?"

Jason's eyes lit up. "You selling?"

"I have a few bikes I'm looking to get rid of. Stop by any time if you want to have a look. I'll give you a deal."

"I'll do that, man. Thanks." Jason kissed Chloe on the side of the head. "Now I really have to get back to work."

They said goodbye and Chloe scooted back to her abandoned tables with a flick of her hand.

"Do you mind?" Jim pushed out the stool next to her with his foot.

"Go ahead." She grabbed a menu from behind the bar as if she'd planned to eat lunch here all along. "Was the rest of your night uneventful?"

His dark gaze drifted away from her face for a few seconds, and then he cleared his throat. "Yeah. You? Were the deputies there all night?"

"I think so. They were there when I went to bed, and a few were there this morning."

"Any news?" He pointed to her menu. "You done with that?"

She slid it across to him. "Autopsy this morning, but I haven't heard anything."

The bartender dropped another menu in front of Scarlett. "Are you two ordering lunch?"

"I am. Give me a minute." Jim ran his finger down the menu and looked at her over the top. "Burgers any good here?"

"You're asking the wrong person. I'm a vegetarian."

He peered down the bar. "They seem popular."

When the bartender returned, Jim ordered a burger and fries, and she stuck to the vegetarian chili, her go-to meal at Sutter's.

"Anything to drink?"

They both ordered water.

When the bartender placed their glasses in front of them, Scarlett followed a bead of moisture running down the outside of her glass with her fingertip. "I wanted to ask you if you were okay after…after your fall last night."

His jaw hardened and a muscle ticked in the corner of his mouth. "The darkness, the excitement, threw me off balance. I usually don't trip over my own feet, believe it or not. Spent enough time in physical therapy to avoid that."

"What happened to your leg?" Taking a sip of water, she avoided his gaze. Would he lash out? Refuse to answer her?

"It broke in a few places and never healed properly."

Okay, so he'd just be vague about it.

"Ouch. Sounds painful. I suppose it happened when you were…over there."

"Uh-huh." He gestured to the bartender. "Can you bring me some ketchup when you get a chance, please?"

She didn't need a brick wall to fall on her to get the hint. Personal stuff—off-limits. "I sure hope the sheriff's department can find out who this guy is and what happened to him—and if he had some kind of beef with his killer."

"I'm sure they'll be able to ID him soon, and most likely it wasn't a random hit. You still need to upgrade the security on your place. Even if you believe you're safe in Timberline, you might want to do a better job protecting your…art."

She narrowed her eyes. "Did I detect a little sarcasm in your tone?"

"What? Not at all." He rolled his water glass between his hands. "I like it."

"The landscape art."

"That, too, but the other stuff…" He shook his head. "Crazy intense."

A warm glow settled in her belly. Usually she didn't care what people thought about her art. She created her work from a personal, imaginative space inside her brain, and if she didn't give expression to those thoughts, her head would explode. It had just been a side bonus that other people, including the art critics, had appreciated her abstract art and paid top dollar for it.

The fact that a man like Jim liked it, got it, made her feel like he got her, that he saw her.

She wanted to get him, too. She felt like she could if he'd let her.

"Veggie chili and Sutter's burger." The bartender dipped beneath the bar and gave them each a silverware setting wrapped in a cloth napkin.

Jim proceeded to drench everything in ketchup.

She pointed a spoon at his fries. "Have some fries with your ketchup."

One corner of his mouth lifted, which was about the closest thing she'd seen to a smile from him.

"One of my many quirks." He bit off the end of a French fry and asked, "Where do you live when you're not spilling your guts on a canvas in Timberline?"

"San Francisco. I have a small place in the city that I share with another artist. When he's gone, I'm usually there and when I'm here, he's in the city."

"Boyfriend?" He took a big bite of his burger.

"What? The artist?" She slipped a spoonful of chili in her mouth to hide her smile, happy that he'd been concerned enough to ask. "Marco is not my boyfriend."

"I was gonna say, tough to have a relationship with someone you hardly see."

"Tough to have a relationship with another artist. Marco and I had a thing once, but it was exhausting—and not in a good way." She winked at him.

He raised one eyebrow and took another bite of his burger.

She zigzagged her spoon through the hot surface of her chili and watched the steam curl up. How had he gotten her to open up while he remained aloof and closemouthed?

"And you? Are you going to settle in Timberline or do you have a home somewhere else?"

"I don't have a home, and I sure as hell don't plan to stay in Timberline."

"Are you here to sell your father's place? I'm sure you know, ever since Evergreen Software moved in, housing prices have shot up."

"I'll probably sell it. Nothing but bad memories attached to the place."

He offered nothing more. Where had he been since being discharged from the army? What was he doing in Timberline? And why did he have the same tattoo as a murder victim?

Jim dragged a napkin across his mouth and tapped her arm. "Incoming."

She jerked her head to the side. "It's Sheriff Musgrove. I guess he's feeling better."

"Is he new?"

"He's new and lazy. More interested in fundraising, but he's been keeping a low profile lately, since he was good friends with Jordan Young."

"Well, he's making a beeline for us, so maybe he has some news from homicide."

As the sheriff made a few stops on his way, Scarlett leaned close to Jim and whispered, "Does it look like everyone is reassured at what he's telling them? Because I'm pretty sure they're asking him about the murder."

"Nobody's screaming and fainting."

Musgrove finally made it to them and positioned himself between their two bar stools. "Trouble just seems to follow you around, doesn't it, Ms. Easton?"

"Me and you both." Scarlett pushed away her bowl. "This is Jim Kennedy. He was with me last night when I stumbled across the body."

The two men shook hands and Jim asked, "News about the murder?"

"Yeah, which is why I came over here when one of the deputies said he saw Ms. Easton at the bar. The fact that you're here, too, is convenient, since I don't have to go out to your place."

"What's the news?"

Musgrove smiled and waved at the bartender. "We identified the victim."

Scarlett slid a glance at Jim. "Who is he?"

"Name's Jeff Kelly, goes by the name of Rusty. He's fifty-one years old and a member of the Lords of Chaos motorcycle gang."

"Club."

"Excuse me?" Musgrove cocked his head, his eyebrows colliding over his nose.

"They prefer to be called a club—the Lords of Chaos Motorcycle Club."

"And how exactly do you know that, Kennedy?"

"Because I was a member—and I knew Rusty."

Chapter Five

Scarlett grabbed the edge of the bar—*LC*. So, those letters stood for Lords of Chaos. She vaguely remembered a bunch of motorcycle-riding tough guys hanging around town, usually with Jim's father and brother. She never realized they were an actual motorcycle gang and that Jim had belonged to it. That explained the tattoo. Explained a lot of other things.

At least he'd owned up to it, but why'd he wait? Why didn't he mention the tattoo earlier, even if he didn't recognize Rusty?

Musgrove must've had the same thought since he fished in his front pocket and asked, "You didn't recognize him last night?"

Jim shrugged. "It was dark. It's been over ten years since I last saw him."

"Have you seen any other members of the… club since you've been back in Timberline?"

"Look, Musgrove. If you want to question me

further, can we do it more formally at the station?" He jerked his thumb over his shoulder. "We're attracting attention."

"Technically, it's not even our case anymore, but I'll give your name to Deputy Collins. He's heading up the investigation for the county's homicide division."

"You do that." Jim grabbed a cocktail napkin and a pen and wrote out his phone number. "Have him give me a call. I can't tell him much. I didn't even realize Rusty was still here. As far as I know, the club doesn't operate in this area anymore."

Musgrove hunched forward. "Is it true the Lords of Chaos were involved in the drug trade here in Timberline?"

"Didn't know much about their business, didn't want to know. I was a teenager and got out when I could."

Musgrove tugged on his earlobe. "Didn't Gary Binder hang out with the club?"

"Gary?" Jim pulled his bottom lip between his teeth. "Nah, kind of a hanger-on. I heard he died in a hit-and-run accident recently."

"We've never found the driver." Musgrove shrugged. "Me? I figured it for an accident, but did you have any contact with Binder since returning?"

Jim spread his hands. "Dead before I arrived."

"All right then, Kennedy." Musgrove stuffed

the napkin with Jim's number into his pocket. "I think Deputy Unger already gave your number to Collins. He'll probably want to talk to you at some point once I tell him you knew Kelly."

"I'm not going anywhere for a while."

Musgrove saluted and walked back through the dining room, glad-handing when he could. When he walked out the front door, Scarlett turned to Jim. "That's why you have the tattoo."

Jim choked on his water. "How do you know about that?"

"When you…fell last night, your shirt hiked up in the back. I saw it then, and I had seen the same tattoo, or at least the same letters, on the neck of the dead man."

"Thought about getting it removed a few times, but it reminds me where I came from and what I have to battle."

She swirled the ice in her water glass. "Is that why you joined the army? To get away from your family?"

"One reason."

"So why'd you come back here?"

"Settle my dad's stuff."

"Liar. We found a dead body together. You can tell me the truth."

He rubbed his knuckles against his sexy stubble. "I came across a news story online about those kidnappings a few months ago. It brought back some…memories."

Not very good memories from the look in his dark, haunted eyes.

"Sounds like you'd rather forget those memories. Why torture yourself by coming back?"

His lips twisted and he smacked the bar as he emitted a noise that sounded suspiciously like a laugh.

"What's funny about that?"

"I wouldn't call being in Timberline and remembering fond times with my old man and my older brother torture—miserable, but not torture."

"Figure of speech, I guess." She waved at the bartender for the check. "Timberline still has a lot of secrets."

"That's because the mystery of the Timberline Trio was never solved." He jerked his thumb over his shoulder at the dining room. "It doesn't affect the newcomers with their shiny tech jobs and their shiny cars in their shiny homes. But for those of us who were kids here at the time, I think it left its imprint."

"I think you're right."

The bartender dropped two separate checks for them. Jim reached for her check at the same time she did.

"Lunch is on me."

As his warm hand curled around hers, a shock flashed through her body and a sharp pain knifed the back of her skull. She squeezed her eyes closed and fought off the visions before they engulfed her.

"Scarlett. What's wrong?"

Her eyelids flew open. Jim's face, etched with worry, was inches from hers. She'd felt electricity from his touch last night, but nothing like this. This had gone beyond the pleasant sensations of attraction and connection she'd experienced before.

She'd dived straight into his psyche and had been overwhelmed by terror and darkness. His terror and darkness? What had his father done to him?

His nostrils flared as he saw something in her eyes. "What just happened?"

"I—I got dizzy for a minute." She slipped her hand from beneath his. "I'm okay, and you really don't have to buy me lunch."

"I absolutely have to buy you lunch now, since it seems as if my touch made you sick to your stomach." He pulled out a few bills from his wallet and put the ketchup bottle on top of the checks and the money.

She gave a halfhearted laugh. "It wasn't that, probably just low blood sugar."

"Do you need something else to drink? A soda? Orange juice?"

His narrowed eyes told her he wasn't buying any of it, but she could at least make good on the pretense.

"Some orange juice is probably just what I need."

When the bartender placed the tall, skinny bar glass full of orange juice in front of her, she downed it. "Ahh, that's better."

"Did you have a chance to call someone about the security measures I suggested?"

"No time yet. Spoke to the deputies this morning, went out to visit my granny and then came into town to pick up few things for her."

"I'm going to that hardware store in the new shopping center out by Evergreen Software. I can pick up a few locks and window rods for you."

"If you don't mind." She snatched a couple of twenties from her wallet. "Use this and let me know if I owe you more."

He stuffed the money in his pocket. "I can drop by later to set things up for you."

"I work during the daylight hours, so catch me when the sun goes down."

They walked out of Sutter's together with several pairs of eyes following them. Word must've gotten around that they'd found Rusty's body. She preferred keeping a low profile when she was in town working, but she'd been the center of attention on her last visit and this one was shaping up to be the same.

"Thanks for lunch and for offering to get my locks."

"No problem." He lifted a helmet from the

backrest of his Harley and straddled the bike. "Thanks for not ratting out my tattoo to the cops."

She parted her lips and then stepped back as he revved the noisy engine of the bike. Of course, he'd realized she had kept that from the sheriff's deputies since she'd admitted she saw the tattoo on Rusty's neck and then had seen a replica on Jim's back.

He revved the Harley's engine again, and then peeled away from the shoulder of the road.

Sighing, she ran her fingers through her hair and tucked the bag of yarn beneath one arm. Time to put Rusty Kelly and Jim Kennedy out of her head and get back to work.

Rusty? That was easy. Jim? That presented a whole different kind of problem.

JIM LOCKED HIS helmet against his bike and grabbed a basket on his way into the hardware store.

Why had Scarlett kept quiet about his tattoo? When she saw it on his back, she must've realized he'd lied to the cops about knowing the dead man, or at least lied about knowing something about him. Had she believed his story about not seeing Rusty's tattoo? Had Musgrove believed his story about not recognizing Rusty last night?

He didn't even know why he'd lied. Habit?

He'd lied so much over the past few years of his life he didn't even know the truth anymore.

He steered his basket down the home security aisle and looked over some sensor lights and cameras. He'd been planning to make a few improvements to Slick's cabin, but security hadn't been one of them—until Rusty turned up dead last night.

Who'd murdered him and why? Could be a barroom fight or some kind of deal gone wrong. But why here in Timberline? As far as he knew, the Lords of Chaos didn't operate in this area anymore, and Rusty didn't have family nearby.

He dropped a few items in his basket and wandered a few aisles over to have a look at the dead bolts. While he was reading the back of a package, a man bumped his arm reaching for a bin of locks.

"Sorry, bro." The man swore and smacked him on the back. "Jim Kennedy. J.T."

Jim's muscles tensed as he drew back. He didn't like people touching him when he didn't see it coming. He really didn't like surprises, and he didn't like being called by his nickname.

The man beside him grinned, his yellowed teeth peeking through a heavy beard. "You don't remember me? It's Chewy. I ran with your old man back in the day."

Jim squeezed the plastic packaging in his

hands until the sides cut into his fingers. What the hell was this, some kind of LOC reunion?

He remembered Chewy—mean SOB with a short-fuse temper, used to smack his woman around.

"Chewy. Yeah, I remember you."

"So the army took your sorry ass, huh?" Chewy had dropped the big paw he'd proffered in a shake when Jim ignored it. "Heard you were some hotshot ranger, a sniper. You always were a good shot, son."

"Tell me, Chewy. Are the Lords of Chaos running a club in Timberline again? You heard about Rusty, right?"

Chewy blinked his small, flat eyes. "Rusty? Haven't seen that fat SOB in a couple of months. What happened to him?"

Jim thought he might be able to catch Chewy in a lie since the sheriff's department hadn't released the identity of the dead body yet. Chewy was as dumb as a box of rocks, but not that dumb.

Jim lifted one shoulder. "Just that he's back in town, too. Saw him the other day."

"I'll be damned. Old Rusty. I'll have to look him up."

"You're staying in town?"

"For a while. Had some good times here." He ran his fingers through his graying beard. "Sorry about Slick. That was a tough break. If any of the Lords had been with him that night, whoever killed him would've been dead meat."

"Yeah. Gotta go." Jim tossed two dead bolts into his basket and rolled away.

Should he bring up Chewy's appearance in town when Deputy Collins questioned him about Rusty? Chewy would clam up or run if the cops came down on him…and Jim just might need the old biker for information.

Jim finished shopping for Scarlett's items, as well as his own, and then secured them in the saddlebags on his bike. He checked the time on his phone. Scarlett would still be working.

He headed for Slick's place—his own now. His brother Dax had dropped off the face of the earth since his release from prison. Jim planned to sell it and all of his dad's bikes once he finished his business in Timberline. He'd never feel at home in that cabin.

He rode his motorcycle to the front door and parked it. Standing by the bike, he sorted Scarlett's stuff into one bag and his in the other. Then he crammed her items back into his saddlebag.

Slick's motorcycles had been in the detached garage for years after his death and nobody had touched them, but nobody had known they were there. Once Jim started advertising them for sale, the cat would be out of the bag and he needed to beef up security.

He'd start with the sensor lights. He dumped his purchases on the kitchen table and then bagged up the pieces he needed for the sensor system.

With the bag under his arm, he trudged down the gravel path to the garage. He dug his key ring from his pocket as he reached the double doors.

"Damn." He kicked the door with his boot.

Too late. Someone had broken off the padlock that held the two doors together.

He loosened the broken lock, letting it fall to the ground. Using his T-shirt to avoid leaving fingerprints, he flicked up the latch and nudged the door open with his foot.

He yanked the chain to turn on the overhead lights and released a sigh. Slick's five Harleys were all where he'd left them when he'd checked them out his first day back.

He entered the garage and scanned the walls, his gaze skimming over the two shotguns mounted in racks and a collection of fishing poles and tackle.

Nothing jumped out at him. Slick had kept plenty of tools in here and God knows what else. He hadn't done an inventory when he'd been in here before. He didn't care if someone robbed Slick blind and Slick wouldn't mind now.

Only the bikes mattered to Jim.

He wandered toward the shotguns and ran a

hand down the long barrel of one. That's one thing he owed the old man. Slick had taught him to shoot—and he'd been a crack shot right from the get-go.

He spent the next few hours setting up the sensor lights on the outside of the garage and fixing the padlock latch. He'd have to think of a better way to lock these doors, and he should probably file a report with the sheriff's department.

He peered at the sky as he returned to the house. The cloud cover hid the setting sun, but it had to be dusk and Scarlett would be done working. Should he bring something more than her locks? Dinner?

At least he knew she hadn't cooled off toward him because of his clumsy fall. His tattoo had freaked her out. Had she believed his story about not seeing Rusty's tattoo or recognizing him in the dark? He wouldn't have believed that lame explanation.

He finished showering and dried off in front of the mirror. Turning his back to the mirror and twisting his head over his shoulder, he could just make out the tail end of the tattoo on his back— the tattoo that ended in the letters *LC*.

Maybe he should've gotten the damned thing removed. At least it had caused some fear among his captors.

He slicked back his wet hair, which almost reached his shoulders. Didn't look much like a ranger these days. He smoothed the pad of his thumb across the thin, white line on his forehead. But he had the battle scars to prove his service.

He shaved and dressed in a pair of jeans and buttoned a red-and-black flannel shirt over his black T-shirt. He grimaced at his reflection in the mirror. "You're dropping off some hardware, Kennedy, not going on a date."

He stuffed his arms into his leather jacket and locked up. He could've walked through the woods to her place, but he was sick of the woods already.

He rode his motorcycle the short mile to Scarlett's place and left it on the edge of the ring of trees sheltering her cabin. He made plenty of noise taking the two steps to the door since he didn't want to startle her and risk getting attacked with a poker.

He used the lion's-head knocker and called out, "Scarlett, it's Jim."

The curtain at the window shifted and he took a step to the side to show himself.

She opened the door. "I thought you'd forgotten about me."

Forget about her? Never.

"You said dusk. I didn't want to disturb your work."

Poking her head outside, she sniffed. "This is night, not dusk."

"Excuse me for missing the nuance." He held up the bag. "These are for you, and I have your change."

She opened the door wider and as the light from the cabin spilled over him, her gaze tracked across his body, igniting a fire in his belly.

Her long, dark lashes fluttered and her chest beneath her tight sweater rose and fell. "C'mon in."

He swung the bag from his fingertips. "Can you install this stuff, or do you know someone who can?"

"I can use a simple screwdriver and hammer, but I draw the line at drills. I don't even think I have a drill."

"I'm sure you can find a handyman to do the job for you."

She shoved her hands in the back pockets of her jeans, which made her sweater fit tighter. "I was kind of hoping you could help me out. I'll pay you…and feed you."

His heart thudded against his chest. All she had to do was look at him like she was doing right now, and he'd hand her the moon on a silver platter.

"Feed me?" He sniffed the air and his mouth watered at the scent of garlic. "Now?"

"I thought it would be more effective to offer you food at the time of the request." Folding her hands in front of her, she batted her eyelashes. "Pretty please?"

He snorted. "You're pulling out all the stops. I'm pretty sure you've never said *pretty please* or batted your eyelashes in your entire life."

She wrinkled her nose. "That bad, huh?"

"Bad, but the food smells great. Is it all vegetarian?"

"Salad, eggplant parmigiana and some penne with meatballs for you. I ordered in from that Italian place in the new shopping center."

"It's a deal."

"Thanks."

She went into the kitchen and he followed, admiring the way her jeans fit her.

She reached into a cupboard and stacked a couple of bowls on top of two plates, and then placed them on the counter. "We'll eat at the counter, if that's okay with you. I rarely use the kitchen table."

"Okay by me." He set the dishes on top of the woven place mats on the counter and pulled out the high chairs beneath it. "Do you want me to put the salad in these bowls?"

"Uh-huh. And…" She spun around, holding a bottle of wine in front of her. "I have wine."

"Just water for me."

She squinted at the label on the bottle. "It's a good year—a cabernet from a Washington winery."

"I don't drink."

"Oh." She hugged the bottle to her chest. "I hope you don't mind if I do."

"Help yourself." He dumped some salad evenly into the two bowls while she opened the wine. He didn't even miss the stuff—except for on nights like the one he'd just had.

After they loaded their plates with food, they sat down at the counter and Jim raised his water glass. "To a drama-free night."

She tapped her glass against his, and the red liquid swirled and caught the light, giving Scarlett's cheeks a rosy glow.

"Did you get much work done this afternoon?" He ripped off a piece of garlic bread and dropped it onto his plate.

"Not really." She waved her fork in the air. "I'd been working on a piece that I'd hoped to finish in the next few weeks, but I started a new project and it distracted me all afternoon. I hate it when that happens."

"You're lucky to have a creative outlet."

"What about you? Now that you're out of the army, what are your plans?"

He stabbed the pasta on his plate and dragged it through the red sauce. She expected an answer. This is how normal people had conversations— give and take. He put down his fork and cleared his throat. "I'd been doing some work with some organizations that help disabled vets."

"Like physical therapy?"

He tapped his head. "The other kind of therapy."

"Wow, that has to be tough."

"For me or for them?"

"For everybody."

"It's no picnic." He hunched forward. "That's why I liked your modern artwork. It looks…therapeutic. I mean, we're looking for all kinds of things to help these guys adjust—pets, music, art."

"Sounds like a great program. Are you going to do that when you're done with…whatever you're doing here?"

"I need more training. I might go back to school. I mean, go to school, since I enlisted in the army after high school."

"Can I give you a piece of advice?" She took a sip of her wine and the ruby liquid stained her lips.

He shifted his gaze from her mouth to her eyes. "Sure."

"You might want to open up a little more."

"I'm supposed to be getting *them* to open up."

She took another swig of wine and tilted her head so that her long hair fell over one shoulder. "You know, you're right. And you're pretty good at that, since you definitely got more out of me than I've gotten out of you."

"I'm not trying to get anything out of you, Scarlett."

"I know, but I've been open with you because…" She ducked her head and stuffed a piece of garlic bread in her mouth.

Garlic or not, he'd kiss her later, anyway. He dragged his gaze from her mouth to her eyes.

"Because?"

"Oh, you know. Because I knew you in high school."

"Yeah, and we were such good friends."

She snorted. "You weren't friends with anyone."

"And you were only friends with the other kids from the rez."

"Couple of social butterflies, I tell ya." She tossed her hair back and laughed.

The knock on Scarlett's door cut across her laugh, and Jim dropped his bread.

"Now what? I guess my toast was a jinx."

She hopped from her stool and stalked toward the front door. He had no intention of letting her open that door by herself, so he dogged her steps and hovered over her shoulder as she peered out the window.

She blew out a noisy breath. "It's Deputy Collins with another officer I don't know."

Jim's muscles tensed, and a rush of adrenaline slammed against his temples. Why would they be out here at this time of night?

Before he could stop her, Scarlett opened the front door. "Do you have any news, Deputy Collins?"

The deputy's eyes widened as he looked past

Scarlett and met Jim's gaze. "I thought you might be here, Kennedy."

Jim widened his stance, placing his weight on his good leg. "Here I am."

Collins placed his hand on his service revolver. "James Kennedy, you're under arrest for the murder of Jeff Kelly."

Chapter Six

Darkness rushed in on Jim and he clenched his fists at his sides. He couldn't be confined. He couldn't let them take him.

The blood raced through his veins and his heart almost pumped out of his chest. If he assaulted the officer and took off, it would be all over for him. He had to get a grip. Innocent men didn't run.

Scarlett's hand closed around his, her cool touch soothing the rage within him.

"What are you talking about, Collins? Jim was here with me last night. We discovered Rusty's body together."

"Ma'am, Ms. Easton, you need to step back, please. We have a warrant for Mr. Kennedy's arrest and I need to read him his rights."

She stamped her foot. "What evidence do you have? This is ridiculous."

Jim dragged in a deep breath. She was on his side. He could do this.

"It's okay, Scarlett. They'll tell me what they have when they get me to the station. If I give you a card, can you call my buddy? He can recommend an attorney in the area for me."

"Jim, this is absurd. You didn't kill anyone."

Her cheeks reddened as if she'd suddenly realized the falsity of that statement spoken to an army ranger sniper.

"I mean, you didn't kill Rusty. Tell him."

"It's okay. I'll have my opportunity."

Collins read him his rights and then asked if he had any weapons on him.

"Not on me." He tilted his head back. "My Glock's in the pocket of my jacket, hanging on that hook."

Collins gestured to the other deputy and then tapped Jim on the shoulder. "Turn around."

Turning, Jim gritted his teeth at the sound of the cuffs jangling behind him. He had to hold everything together so the cops wouldn't have him for resisting arrest, even though every fiber in his body was screaming at him to fight. He had to tamp down his rising rage.

Breathe. Think. Reason.

"Can you get my wallet out of my pocket and give it to Scarlett?"

Collins patted him down and removed the wallet. He handed it to Scarlett.

Jim met Scarlett's frantic gaze with his own steady one. "There's a card in there for Ken Stucken. Give him a call and tell him what happened. Tell him I need an attorney."

Scarlett's hands shook as she rifled through his wallet. "I found it."

She held up the card and he nodded, giving her a half smile as Collins and the other deputy marched him away from her house, through the trees to their squad car. They couldn't have much evidence, since he hadn't done it, but they wouldn't tell him anything until they got him to the station. He knew how it worked.

Jim kept his gaze pinned to the passing scenery out the car window and took deep breaths. If he had to spend the night in jail, he had doubts he could handle it. The deputies would probably transfer him to the psych ward before the night was over, giving them even more reason to believe he'd killed Rusty.

They took him to the sheriff's station in town. Cody Unger wasn't on duty when they arrived, but this wasn't the local deputy's rodeo, anyway.

Jim asked, "Is Sheriff Musgrove here?"

"Not here," Collins said, and cleared his throat. "But we notified him of the warrant."

Collins nudged him in the back toward a glass-enclosed interview room. "We're going to question you before we book you, Kennedy.

You have a right to have your attorney present during questioning."

"I'll waive that right for now. I'm too curious to find out what you think you have on me."

Collins shoved open the door and pointed to a chair. "Coffee?"

"No, thanks. Let's just get to it."

The other deputy set up a camera as Jim awkwardly sank to a chair, his hands still cuffed behind him.

"Do you need to keep me handcuffed?"

Collins took in Jim's frame and then studied his face. "No."

Free of the cuffs, Jim's heart rate returned to something close to normal. He rubbed his wrists. "Why did you arrest me? What evidence do you have?"

The other deputy reached into a box and pulled out a plastic bag. He tossed it onto the table in front of Jim. "Recognize it?"

Jim peeled his tongue from the roof of his dry mouth. "It's my old man's hunting knife."

"It was also used to stab Rusty Kelly."

"Let me guess. My fingerprints are on the knife."

"Your fingerprints and Rusty's blood."

"That's an incriminating combination." Jim folded his arms across his chest and slumped in the metal chair, stretching his legs in front of him.

Collins smoothed the crinkles from the plastic bag. "One you can explain?"

"My fingerprints are on the knife because it was in my dad's shed. The shed is a detached wooden structure that he used as a garage for his motorcycles. I was in there last week and moved some things around. I remember handling the knife, which was on the tool bench."

"That explains the fingerprints."

"I just discovered today that someone broke into the garage. It has double doors that lock together with a simple padlock."

"Did you file a report?"

"No, but I called the station. I couldn't tell if anything was missing, so the deputy... Stevens, asked if I wanted to make a report but I declined. Deputy Stevens—ask him."

Collins snapped his fingers. "Jenkins, find Deputy Stevens to verify."

"There's also my alibi."

"Alibi?"

"I was with Scarlett Easton when she found the body."

"Kelly was stabbed before you arrived at Ms. Easton's."

"How much earlier before we discovered his body? I have an alibi for that, too."

"What's your timeline?"

"I ate dinner in town at the Miner's Inn and left around eight o'clock. Used a credit card. I had trouble starting my bike, and I talked to a man named Terry while I was trying to get it to work. That was right outside the Miner's Inn, right in front of the window, so plenty of people saw me. I didn't leave until about eight forty-five or eight fifty. When I got to my place, I thought I heard some noises so I parked my bike and went for a walk in the woods. I got to Scarlett's place around nine fifteen or nine twenty. She can vouch for that."

Collins had been eyeing Jim's face and hands during his narrative without one interruption. Even now, he just nodded.

Jim dragged in a breath. "So, if I stabbed Rusty, I would've had to do it in a short time span, getting the knife, locating him, stabbing him without getting a drop of his blood on my clothes since I wouldn't have had time to change before going to Scarlett's."

"And all this is going to check out?" Collins folded his hands on the table between them.

"It'll all check out." Jim sat up in his chair and faced the camera. "Now if you want to ask me any more questions, you'll have to wait for my attorney."

Jim knew he had a rock-solid alibi. That didn't concern him. What did was the fact that someone had tried to frame him for murder—and he had a feeling it was all related to what happened to him twenty-five years ago.

WHEN THE PHONE RANG, Scarlett pounced on it before the call could drop off, grabbed her purse and ran outside.

She reached the end of her drive and answered, out of breath. "Is Jim going to have to spend the night in jail? What do they have? What can I do to help?"

Wade Lewiston, the attorney Jim's friend had recommended, clicked his tongue. "They haven't even booked him, Scarlett. He's waiting in an interview room while they check out his alibi."

"If they ask me, I can tell them straight out, no way could he have stabbed someone and then appeared on my doorstep without a smidgen of blood on him."

"From what I understand, his timeline is pretty tight. They're not going to be able to pin this on him. He even phoned in about the garage break-in. He's covered."

"D-do you need to come out?"

"I don't think so. He's not answering any more questions for now. He wanted me to ask you if you can pick him up at the station when they release him."

"Of course I can. I'm on my way right now."

"You might want to wait, Scarlett. The deputies are still looking into his alibi."

"I'm not waiting any longer. This is ridiculous."

"Up to you. If Jim needs anything else, have him give me a call."

"How about a lawsuit? Can he sue the sheriff's department?"

"'Fraid not. His fingerprints were on the murder weapon, and that weapon belonged to him. The deputies had just cause to bring him in."

"Okay, okay." She ran a hand through her hair. "I'm going there now, anyway."

"Good night and good luck. Call me if there's a hitch."

Scarlett hit the key fob and the lights of her car blinked once. "Will do."

"One more thing, Scarlett."

"What?"

"Just be careful."

"Careful?" She slid behind the wheel of her car, glancing in her rearview mirror. "Of what? Jim didn't do it."

"That's not what I meant."

"What did you mean?"

"There's a murderer loose in Timberline, and for whatever reason he dumped the man near your cabin and tried to frame Jim. Be careful."

The hair on the back of her neck quivered. Like she needed reminding. "I'll be careful. Thanks for getting back to me so quickly tonight."

"Anything for a fellow vet—especially one like Jim Kennedy."

Before she had a chance to ask him why Jim was so special, he ended the call.

By the time she pulled into the parking lot of the sheriff's station, her aching muscles were screaming at her. She'd made the drive clutching the steering wheel and sitting on the edge of her seat.

She felt a particular urgency biting at her heels—something telling her that if she didn't get Jim out tonight, he would never get out.

She scrambled from the car and jogged to the station entrance. Deputy Stevens looked up from behind the front desk.

"I'm here to pick up Jim Kennedy. Are you done harassing him?"

Stevens's mouth dropped open. "H-his fingerprints were on the murder weapon, which belonged to his father."

"And he had alibis about a mile long."

Stevens held up his hands. "This was county's arrest. Don't jump on me."

"Well, is he done?" She wedged a hand on her hip and tapped the toe of her boot.

"I think so. They'll bring him up when they're ready. Deputy Collins didn't even book him, so there's no paperwork to process."

Scarlett wheeled around and paced to the other side of the room. After about fifteen minutes of handwringing and peppering Stevens with questions, she froze when she heard a door open down the hall.

The distinctive tone of Jim's low voice carried across the room, and Scarlett rushed to the front desk.

Jim and Deputy Collins, deep in conversation, came down the hallway. Jim jerked his head up, his eyes widening briefly.

"What are you doing here?"

"I'm here to pick you up. I spoke to Wade Lewiston earlier this evening. He said you told him to have me pick you up."

"I was going to call you. Didn't want you hanging around here."

"And I didn't want *you* hanging around here any longer than you had to." Her gaze shifted to Collins and she pursed her lips. "Everything straightened out?"

Jim massaged the back of his neck. "Almost everything. I'd still like to know who stole Slick's knife—a knife that conveniently had my fingerprints on it."

"We want to know the same thing." Deputy Collins shook Jim's hand. "We'll keep you updated. Sorry about the mix-up."

"You were just doing your job."

"Your stuff." Stevens pushed out of his chair and grabbed a box from a credenza. He held out the box to Jim and shook it. "We unloaded your weapon, but your license and permit checked out. You're free to take it."

Jim placed the box on a desk and pocketed his wallet and keys. He shoved the gun into his jacket pocket and dumped the bullets into his palm. "Someone's going to come out tomorrow to dust the garage for prints?"

"Yeah, we'll call first."

Jim held the door open for her and when she stepped outside, the cool air stung her hot cheeks. She rounded on Jim. "How could you be so polite? They arrested you. They handcuffed you and dragged you into the station like some dirtbag criminal."

He put his hands on her shoulders. "They had a murder weapon with my prints on it. What do you want them to do, ignore the evidence?"

His words sounded reasonable, but his hands felt unsteady. He dropped them quickly.

"You're a better person than I am. I would've been livid. You were with me when I stumbled across the body. I wouldn't have noticed if you'd had blood all over you? The cops showed up almost immediately after. They wouldn't have noticed any other blood besides what you had on your hands?"

"It's over, Scarlett, at least this part."

"What does that mean and why is everyone talking in riddles tonight?"

"I wanna know if someone tried to set me up for Rusty's murder."

"Why would someone do that?"

He nudged her back. "Let's get in the car."

As she grabbed the driver's-side handle, he asked, "Are you okay after drinking that wine?"

"Are you kidding? I barely got started on that bottle before we were rudely interrupted." She yanked open the car door. "I plan to finish it off now."

On the way back to her place, Jim told her about the interview and how the deputies had tracked down his alibis.

"I was lucky I hadn't been sitting at home alone the night of Rusty's murder."

"Maybe something drew you to my place last night for a reason."

"Whatever it was, it saved me a lot of trouble."

Turning down the road that led to her place and his, she slid a glance his way. "Do you want me to drop you off at your cabin or do you want to come back to mine and finish dinner?"

"I thought we finished dinner."

"I bought a cheesecake for dessert."

"I lost my appetite, but I have to pick up my bike."

The car bumped and jostled as she drove up the access road to her cabin. She backed into the spot she'd had cleared for her car when she first bought the place and killed the engine. "Are you sure you don't want to come in? I have the card you gave me inside and your wallet."

"If you're sure. It's late."

"I'm still wired." She shoved open the car door. "And I still have a bottle of wine to polish off."

He followed her down the path through the trees, both of them leading with the lights on their phones.

"You should install some lights along this pathway, too. It's like the blind leading the blind out here."

"I guess I'm used to it now."

She tripped and Jim caught her around the waist.

"You're used to it, huh? Tell you what, you earned more of my services by calling my buddy and contacting that attorney, Lewiston. I'll work on setting up some lights out here, too."

She'd like to earn more of his services than getting a few lights installed.

She cleared her throat. "Do you think there's going to be any more trouble? I was kind of hoping someone targeted Rusty specifically."

"I think he was the target, but I have a funny feeling about that knife. Why my knife and my fingerprints?"

"Where'd they find it?" She opened her front door and left it open for Jim to follow her inside.

"On the road between our two places, a runner found it. It's probably the same location where the killer dumped Rusty."

"I think I'll have that wine now." She tossed

her purse onto a chair and made a beeline for the kitchen. She uncorked the bottle she'd left on the counter and poured a healthy amount into the glass she'd used earlier.

She raised her glass. "Are you sure you don't want some? I have beer in the fridge, too."

"I'm good." He perched on the arm of the sofa. "I saw someone else from the old life today."

"Who?"

"His name's Charles Swanson. We called him Chewy." He rubbed the back of his neck. "I told the deputies about him."

"Do you think he might've had something to do with Rusty's murder?" She took a gulp of wine and welcomed the warm feeling spreading to her chest.

"Seems suspicious that he's in town at the same time as Rusty and then Rusty turns up dead."

"If the Lords of Chaos want to knock each other off, they can have at it—as long as they do it far away from me." She covered her mouth. "Present company excluded, of course."

His dark brows collided over his nose. "I'm not one of them."

"I know. I didn't mean…"

"Were you here when Gary Binder was killed in that hit-and-run?" He pinched the bridge of his nose and squeezed his eyes shut.

"What does that have to do with anything?"

"Were you?"

"I was here. The cops never made an arrest, and it just about destroyed his mother. She stuck with him through all the ups and downs—the drug use, the arrests—and then just when he started getting his life together, it's snuffed out by a hit-and-run driver."

"Binder was cooperating with the police on the Timberline Trio case, wasn't he?"

"Was he? I don't know that I'd call it cooperating. I don't think he had much to offer."

Jim jumped up from the sofa, one hand clutching his hair. "He was on the fringes of the drug trade here in Timberline."

"The drug trade? Is that what Agent Harper was looking into when he was out here investigating the Timberline Trio case?"

"Harper was the FBI agent assigned to the cold case?" Jim stroked the bristle on his chin.

"Yeah. He was going to interview Gary but never got the chance."

"That's convenient. I wonder if Rusty or Chewy was in town then." He took a few steps and then braced one hand against the mantel. "Can I have some water, please?"

Walking into the kitchen, she glanced over her shoulder at his flushed face. "Are you okay?"

"I'm... I'm..." His head fell forward and he sucked in a breath.

"Jim?" Scarlett's heart pounded as she stuck a glass beneath the tap and filled it with water. He let out a groan and then crashed to the floor.

Chapter Seven

"Jim!" She dropped the water glass in the sink where it shattered and she stumbled into the living room.

She crouched beside Jim, on his side, his knees drawn to his chest. Pressing her hand against his clammy brow, she asked, "Jim, can you hear me?"

His eyeballs rolled behind closed lids, and she brushed his hair back from his face. If he didn't open his eyes in two seconds and talk to her, she'd run outside to call 911. But she didn't want to leave him.

She undid the buttons on his shirt, her hand skimming the hot flesh at his neck. The temperature had to be low sixties in here. Why was he burning up?

His eyelids flickered and she caught the gleam from his dark eyes. "Are you coming around? I'm going to get that water."

She grabbed a pillow from the sofa and tucked it beneath his head.

She took off for the kitchen and filled another glass full of water, ignoring the broken glass in the sink. When she returned to Jim, his breathing was less shallow, his color less pale.

She punched up the pillow behind his head, and held the glass to his dry lips. "Can you take some water? Should I call 911?"

He turned his head, and she put the glass down on the fireplace. As he held up one hand, she grabbed it with her own. Immediately a flow of energy coursed through her body and she jerked back without releasing Jim's hand.

Dread soaked into her skin and it felt as if something was waiting for her just around the corner. Holding her breath, she braced for the terror. She squeezed Jim's hand harder. Her heart thudded in her chest.

Jim ripped his hand from hers and struggled to sit up. "I'm all right."

While she blinked her eyes, Jim grabbed the water and downed it. "I'm fine. It's nothing. Come back."

Her hand snaked up the column of her throat. How had he known? What had he seen in her face?

"I'm here, of course. What just happened?"

"You tell me." He sat up fully, his back against the fireplace, his flannel shirt gaping open, exposing the black T-shirt beneath that clung to the muscles of his broad chest.

"Y-you fell to the floor. You were unresponsive, with shallow breathing and clammy skin. What was that, Jim? You don't seem exactly panicked about it."

"That's because it's happened before. The… attacks or seizures stopped for a while but have started up again since I've been in Timberline."

"Seizures? What causes them? I assume you've been to see a doctor." She crossed her legs beneath her, folding her hands in her lap.

"It's post-traumatic stress. It's been treated. I was on medication for a while—didn't like it."

"Did it help?"

"It reduced the attacks, but I'd rather feel my feelings, not stuff them away."

"You said they stopped?"

"Until I came here." He cradled the glass in his hands, running his thumb along the rim.

"Why? What is it about this place? Is it the stuff you went through with your father?"

"Some of it." He hunched forward. "I'd rather hear about what you feel when you touch me."

Heat washed into her cheeks. "Wh-what do you mean?"

"I'm not talking about the sexual chemistry, although who are we kidding?" He dragged a hand through his hair. "I mean the other stuff—the way you act like I've given you an electric shock when you grab my hand. I've affected different women in different ways, but I've never encountered that response before. What's going on, Scarlett?"

She took a shaky breath and rose to her feet. "I need the rest of my wine for this conversation."

"Let me get it for you." He pushed to his feet and swayed before grabbing the edge of the mantel. He held out his hand as she leaned toward him. "I'm okay. I need to move."

He swept up the empty water glass and walked into the kitchen, his limp more pronounced than usual. "You have broken glass in your sink."

"Yeah, I dropped it when you collapsed in my living room."

"Sorry I scared you." He returned with her wine and more water for himself. "I should've realized I was susceptible after the arrest."

She took the wineglass from his hand and their fingers brushed. She felt nothing but desire this time.

She sank to a chair and he took the chair across from her, resting his forearms on his knees, holding his glass with two hands.

Closing her eyes, she took a sip of wine. "You know about my heritage."

"You're Quileute."

"Yes, but our tribe has shamans, like many others. I'm convinced we don't have greater numbers of people with these sensitivities than the general population, but it's something we identify and foster within our tribe. And I do believe extrasensory perceptions run in families—and it runs in ours."

"Your granny was a shaman. I remember that."

"You do?" A swell of pleasure crested through her body.

"I remember a lot about you, Scarlett Easton."

His dark eyes burned into hers and she felt like that schoolgirl peeking at his geometry test again.

She shook her head. "Anyway, I have these abilities, too."

"And when you touch me…what? You see my future?"

"More like your past."

Jim bolted upright. "You see into my past?"

"Not exactly." She tapped her wineglass with her fingernail. "It's so hard to explain. I'm not really seeing anything real. I have visions, experience feelings, sensations."

"No wonder you recoil every time you grab my hand." He lifted one eyebrow. "It's enough to give a guy a complex."

She stared into the shimmering surface of her wine. "What is it I'm experiencing, Jim? There's so much darkness, so much terror and something else…something unknown."

"Where do I begin?" He rolled the glass of water between his hands.

Leaning forward in her chair, she tapped his bad leg. "Why don't you start with this? What happened to your leg? Why do you suffer from PTSD?"

"I was captured by the enemy, kept in a confined space, tortured and threatened with beheading on a daily basis."

Gasping, Scarlett folded her arms over her stomach. "Wh-what did they do to your leg?"

"They broke it and never set it. It healed improperly." He shrugged. "I could endure the physical pain more than the psychological. Seeing people I'd grown to like and respect being dragged out and tortured and in some cases beheaded—" his jaw hardened "—was worse than the physical torture."

"How'd you get out?"

"Three of us escaped—me, a Dutch journalist and a German contractor. Just like a prison break, we tunneled out of there. We had help from a few locals who got us across the border."

"I can't even imagine." She collapsed back in her chair. "Was it in the news?"

"My companions were in the news. The U.S. Army kept me out of it, had managed to keep my capture out of the headlines, too. I'd been in Syria on a classified mission. Technically, I was never there."

"You'd worked through the PTSD until you came back here to Timberline?"

"Pretty much."

"Then why come back here? Your memories of home, of family, are hardly healing material."

"I want to deal with everything in my past, put it to rest so it can't come up and sabotage me later." He stretched his legs in front of him, almost touching the toes of her boots. "When I saw the Wyatt Carson copycat kidnappings in the news and then read that the TV show *Cold Case Chronicles* was going to do a segment on the Timberline Trio, I took it as a sign."

"I helped the host of *Cold Case Chronicles*, Beth St. Regis. She thought she was one of the Timberline Trio, which turned out not to be the case. I know you don't think you were one of the Timberline Trio, so what's your connection to the case?"

"I wasn't one of the Timberline Trio, but I could've been."

"What are you talking about? Three kids were kidnapped—Kayla Rush, Heather Brice and Stevie Carson, the only boy and Wyatt's brother."

"During that same time, a man appeared in my bedroom and tried to put a foul-smelling rag over my mouth. I fought him off and made enough of a commotion that it woke up my old man from his drunken stupor in the living room."

"Oh, my God. I never heard about any of that. Did he run away when your father got there?"

"No." Jim massaged his temples. "That's just

it. Slick stopped him, but then they moved to the other room and Slick told me to go back to bed. Of course, I didn't. I listened at my bedroom door while the two of them argued. It's like they knew each other and Slick was trying to weasel his way out of something."

"That's crazy, Jim." She picked up her wineglass and took another sip. She could use a shot of whiskey about now, but Jim obviously didn't drink and she didn't want to scare him off.

"After he left, Slick came into my room and I pretended to be asleep, but he caught up with me the next day. Told me if I ever told anyone about what happened, he'd give me a beating I'd never forget. I believed him."

Her heart hurt for the boy Jim had been, and she placed her hand on her chest. "Was that the end of it?"

"No. Kayla Rush was kidnapped a week later, and then Stevie Carson and finally Heather Brice."

She swallowed. "Do you think the Timberline Trio kidnappings were related to your botched kidnapping?"

"Yes. I don't know how or why, but I've always felt it—" he pounded a fist against his chest "—here. That means Slick had something to do with the Timberline case or he knew something about it."

"What about your older brother?"

"He was fifteen at the time. I'm not sure he'd know anything."

"Have you ever spoken to him about it?"

"Until recently, he was in prison for drug trafficking as part of the Lords of Chaos. I know he's out of the joint because he dropped me a line through the army, but we haven't been in touch since."

"That might be a place to start."

"I'm hoping Slick's cabin turns up some clues."

"Or…"

"No." He pushed up from the chair and grabbed her empty wineglass from the table next to her. "You're not going to help me by reading my mind or getting me into some sort of hypnotic dream state. I don't need that. I remember exactly what happened twenty-five years ago."

"If not me, how about help from a therapist?" She waved her hands. "I don't mean with repressed memories, but getting treatment for your PTSD."

"I had some of that before. I figured I'd kicked those spells—or whatever you want to call them—for good, only to have them crashing back on me in good old Timberline."

"I know a good therapist. Her name's Dr. Shipman, and she practices in Port Angeles. I can give you her number."

"I'll take it."

Yawning, Jim stretched his arms over his head

and she got a full view of his muscles flexing beneath his T-shirt. But the man had more than sexy packaging.

His life story had given her a whole new appreciation for his fortitude and bravery. He'd faced enough demons to last most people a hundred lifetimes and yet here he was back in Timberline to confront another.

He rubbed a hand across his mouth. "That's the most I've talked since my debriefing. I don't expect you to care or want to get involved with any of this."

"I kind of didn't have a choice, did I? For whatever reason, Rusty decided to make his way to my cabin after someone stabbed him and dumped him on the road."

"I hope to God it was just a coincidence that led him to you. The Lords of Chaos?" He sliced one finger across his throat. "Not anyone you want to be involved with."

"You survived."

"Only by enlisting in the army. Otherwise, I'd be dead like Slick or an ex-con like Dax."

"I didn't even realize you were a member of a motorcycle gang. How far were you into it?"

"Further than I wanted to be. It's like a legacy—club membership is handed down from generation to generation. To escape is to turn your back on your family and your friends. I had to do both."

"You never regretted it?"

"Never. In the army, with my unit, I found another family." He flicked the card he'd given her earlier, which listed the name she'd called to get to the attorney in Seattle. "This guy's someone I can count on in any crisis."

"You're lucky."

Twisting his wrist, he glanced at his watch. "It's late. You've done more than enough tonight. At this rate, I owe you a remodel."

"I might take you up on that." She stood up beside him and shoved her hands in her pockets to keep from touching him. "Are you sure you're okay? That seizure was pretty scary."

"It's more like a blackout, and the medical doctors tell me it's all in my head and there's nothing physically wrong with me...except my messed-up leg. I'm all right, but I will take Dr. Shipman's number if you have it handy."

"Give me your cell number and I'll send it to you that way."

He recited his cell phone number to her and she forwarded Dr. Shipman's number to him in a text.

She held up her phone. "Not sure that text is going through, but it will eventually."

"When are you going to get that landline?"

"I'll get to it."

"You can't keep running outside down to the road to make calls in case of emergencies."

"Funny thing is?" She tossed her phone on the kitchen counter. "I never had any emergencies before people started digging into the old Timberline case."

"Wyatt Carson started it all by kidnapping those three kids in an attempt to duplicate the original crime, and then positioning himself as the hero by rescuing them."

"You're right. That put Timberline back in the news and prompted Beth St. Regis to make a pilgrimage out here, and now you. I'm glad Beth got her answers and I hope you do, too, but digging into all this old stuff is stirring up trouble."

Jim reached her front door and grabbed the handle. Without turning around, he said, "Maybe you should go back to San Francisco, Scarlett."

"Maybe I have a stake in this myself."

He leaned his back against the door, facing her. "What would that be?"

"The Timberline Trio kidnappings affected me, too."

"I think they affected all of us who grew up here."

"It's more than that. I'm sure you've heard the rumors about the Quileute legends and how some of the elders believed it was a creature from our own myths who kidnapped those children."

"I remember a little about that."

"Well, I remember a lot. We were forbidden from discussing the case. It was all hush-hush."

"Maybe the elders didn't want to frighten the kids on the reservation."

She snorted. "They scared us all the time with those old stories, mostly to keep us in line. This was different. Any time the older kids talked about the kidnappings, they were shushed. The parents wouldn't even discuss it. It was all strange, and Granny wanted no part of it."

"What do you mean by that?"

"Granny is a more powerful shaman than I am, or at least she was. With children missing, I would've thought she'd offer her services to the sheriff's department, even if they ended up scoffing at her, but she wanted to distance herself from that case."

"What are you saying?"

"I don't even know, but I'd be happy if the case were solved and everyone could put their demons to rest."

"I don't know if I'm going to solve the case, Scarlett. I just want to understand my part in it, my father's part in it."

As she hung on the door, he stepped into the glow of light on the porch. "Just be careful. I'll stop by tomorrow to install those new locks for you."

"After lunch is a good time for me."

"See you then, and thanks for…everything."

She watched him disappear into the trees surrounding her cabin and listened for the growl of his Harley's engine. Then she closed the door and rested her forehead against it.

What was it about this damned case that it kept haunting her, insinuating itself into her life? Now she had an even greater reason for seeing it solved—because Jim Kennedy would never be available until it was.

She banged her head against the door—not that she needed him to be available. She didn't need a complicated man like Jim in her life. She didn't need to take care of him or rescue him. She was done rescuing men—most didn't want it and ended up dragging her down with them, anyway.

She returned to the kitchen, corked the rest of the wine and washed out her glass. If Jim abstained from drinking, maybe he was an alcoholic. Even if he was in recovery, she didn't want to go down that road again.

After cleaning up, she lay in bed staring at the ceiling. Despite that second glass of wine, she couldn't get to sleep. Jim's story haunted her. How did anyone survive something like that without cracking up? Death had been hanging over his head on a daily basis. No wonder peeling back the bandage on his painful childhood didn't scare him. What would?

A relationship with someone. She could see that in his eyes, too. She didn't even need her special powers for that.

A yellow glow peeped in from the curtains, and she looked at the clock radio beside her bed. How long had she been lying awake? The sun did not rise at three in the morning. Even if it did, the cloudy sky rarely allowed it to shine through like this.

She caught her breath and stumbled out of bed, yanking the curtains back from the window.

Her eyes widened at the view—flames danced among the trees outside her cabin, sending a cloud of black smoke into the air.

With her heart pounding, she ran into the living room and grabbed her purse and yanked her phone off the charger. Jim had been right. She needed to make this call now but had to run out to the road to call 911.

She rushed to the front door and threw it open. Tripping to a stop, she smacked a hand over her mouth.

The blaze had spread to the trees in front of the cabin, too. She jumped off the porch and turned in a circle. Fire licked at the entire copse of trees surrounding her place.

She was trapped—and someone had made sure of it.

Chapter Eight

The pounding in his head drove Jim outside. He should've never spilled his guts to Scarlett. He needed to keep his demons to himself. He'd seen the horror and the pity in her eyes...and something else. Maybe it was that something else that kept drawing him to her.

As he headed into the clearing around his cabin, he sniffed the air. The acrid smell of smoke permeated the mist.

Tilting his head back, he scanned the dark sky. An orange glow appeared over the top of the tree line—in the direction of Scarlett's cabin.

He scrambled back inside, grabbed his jacket and keys and jumped onto his bike. The smoke grew thicker and he could see dark clouds of it billowing up to the sky the closer he got to Scarlett's place.

He roared past her mailbox onto the access road leading to her cabin and stopped well behind the ring of trees that encircled her property. The ring of trees that was burning up like kindling in a fireplace.

The flames could easily jump from the trees to her cabin given their proximity to each other.

Was she even awake? He called 911 on his phone for the second time in three days. The emergency operator assured him that the fire engines would be on their way in minutes.

Scarlett didn't have minutes.

He edged around the fire to see if he could get in around the side, but the wall of flames continued around her entire property.

How the hell had that happened?

He scoured the ground and found a long stick. Then he covered his head with his leather jacket and beat a path through the fire.

He stumbled into the clearing and dragged in a smoky breath.

As he peered at the front door of the cabin, it burst open and Scarlett appeared on the porch like a ghost, a white T-shirt floating around her.

He yelled, "Scarlett, you need to get out of here."

"Oh, my God. The fire's everywhere. I couldn't breathe outside anymore. How did you get through?"

"Very carefully." He charged past her into the cabin. "We could use some wet towels. The fire department is on its way."

She grabbed three towels from the floor and held them up as they dripped water. "I already thought of that. I was going to put these against the doors."

"We're going to use them to get through the burning copse instead. As the tree branches burn and break away, it's actually creating some space." He grabbed one of the sopping wet towels from her. "Put this over your head. Wrap the other one around your arms. I'll lead you out."

"What about you?"

"This wet towel is more than I had coming in. I'll be fine."

When they got to the line of fire, Jim draped the towels over Scarlett's head and face. "Just hang on to me and I'll get you through the fire."

He tucked the other towel around her arms and hands and created a tent over his head with the third towel.

Using his stick again, he beat out a swath through the smoldering areas of brush with Scarlett clinging to his back.

They broke free to the clearing just as the fire engines came wailing up the road.

"Move to the road, Scarlett. I'm going to back my bike out of here."

"What about my car?"

"Leave it. You won't be able to get it past the fire trucks."

Scarlett ran toward her mailbox as the first fire

truck careened to a stop. It backed up and then rolled up the access road, stirring up the gravel and breaking branches as it squeezed through.

Jim pushed his bike up the road, and Scarlett followed him. A second fire engine rolled onto the scene, followed by a cop car.

Deputy Stevens jumped from the car almost before he parked it.

"Everyone okay? Ambulance on the way."

Jim squeezed the back of Scarlett's neck. "How's your breathing, Scarlett?"

She coughed. "It's been better."

"I'm fine. EMTs should see to her first."

Scarlett pointed to his arm. "You got burned."

"It's nothing. Just a few embers hit me. You?"

She brushed her hand down her bare leg below her knee. "Same. Feels like a few hot spots, but nothing major."

"We'll let the EMTs decide that." Stevens jerked his chin toward the oncoming ambulance.

Jim asked, "Is Sheriff Musgrove coming?"

Stevens shook his head. "The sheriff's out of town today—on business. Let's get Scarlett to the ambulance."

Taking Scarlett's hand, Jim led her to the ambulance and waved at the EMT exiting the vehicle. "She needs assistance. Possible smoke inhalation and burns."

The EMT opened the back of the ambulance. "Anyone else injured?"

"No."

Scarlett tugged on his shirt. "Check him out, too."

"Have a seat, ma'am."

Scarlett sat inside the van on the edge, while the other EMT pulled out some equipment.

Jim eyed Scarlett's flimsy T-shirt, now soaking wet from the towels. "Can you get her a blanket?"

Once Scarlett had a blanket draped around her shoulders, Jim touched her knee. "Are you okay here? I'm going to have a look at the fire."

"Go. Let me know if it reached the cabin. All my work is in there."

As Jim loped back to the fire engines, he tilted his head back. A helicopter had swooped into the area and dumped its flame retardant material onto the tree line behind Scarlett's cabin. They wouldn't want this fire to spread to the rest of the forest.

He approached the firefighter giving orders. "How's it going? Is the residence safe?"

The fireman tipped back his helmet. "Cabin is safe. We have the fire mostly contained in the front here and the helicopter should take care of the back. We'll be here for another few hours, though, and investigators are going to want to come in the morning. Do you live in the cabin?"

"My friend does—the woman."

"Is she okay?"

"Getting treatment now."

"She should find another place to bunk tonight—or at least for the rest of the morning. She's not getting back inside for the time being."

"She can stay at my place down the road. Do you need us for anything?"

"You can leave." He pointed to Deputy Stevens standing by his patrol car. "Check with the deputy over there so he can get your name and number. The investigators will want to talk to you tomorrow."

Jim dipped his head and waited until Stevens got off the phone. "I'm going to take Scarlett to my cabin. She doesn't have her phone or anything, so you can send the arson investigators to me tomorrow when they want to talk to her."

"Arson?" Stevens pocketed his phone. "Who said anything about arson?"

"I just did. Did you see that fire? It didn't hop over from the forest. It didn't start on one side of the cabin and burn in a line. Somebody set fire along the line of trees ringing Scarlett's cabin. I don't know if that person wanted this to look like a natural occurrence, but he failed."

"If that's true, the investigators will figure it out." Stevens jerked his thumb over his shoulder. "Is Scarlett okay?"

"I'm gonna go find out right now."

Scarlett hopped off the back of the ambulance

when he approached, tugging the blanket around her body. "Did my cabin burn?"

"Nope. Did you notice that helicopter? It's keeping the flames at bay in the back. The fire chief told me your cabin was safe."

"Thank God." She covered her eyes with one hand. "Can I go back inside? I'm assuming I can't stay."

"You can't stay and you can't go back inside."

"My purse. I left my purse, my phone—" she plucked the wet T-shirt away from her body "—my clothes."

"It's not safe, Scarlett. What did the EMT say?"

"I'm fine. They want to have a look at you." She held out her arms and the blanket slid to the ground. "They put some ointment on my burns, but they're not serious."

One of the EMTs came around from the front of his vehicle. "Sir, we'd like to test your lung capacity and treat your burns."

Jim shrugged out of his leather jacket. "Here, Scarlett. Put this on and wrap that blanket around your waist."

Not that he didn't enjoy the view through the wet T-shirt clinging to her body, but the fire had done nothing to heat up the gray skies and cool temps of the early morning.

Jim followed the EMT's instructions but

stopped short of allowing him to dab ointment on his burns. "I can do that."

The EMT dropped a sample tube of the burn ointment into Jim's palm. "You two are lucky you got through the fire line, but you probably could've waited it out in the cabin until the fire department arrived."

Jim jumped off the ambulance. "I don't like leaving my fate in the hands of others. Any follow-up treatment recommended for Scarlett?"

"Just watch those burns for any signs of infection, take some ibuprofen for the pain, if necessary, and report any breathing problems immediately."

"That sounds easy enough." Scarlett joined them, hugging his leather jacket around her body.

Looked a lot better on her than it did on him.

Jim held up the ointment. "Did you get one of these?"

She shook her head, and Jim tossed the tube to her. "Stick that in the pocket of the jacket and let's get out of here."

"Not many places I can go looking like this." She spread her arms wide and the jacket opened. He kept his gaze pinned to her face, even though the wet T-shirt molded to her breasts.

"My place. Didn't I make that clear before? I'll take you back to my cabin—as long as you're not expecting some kind of art gallery like you have."

She dropped the blanket back inside the ambulance. "I'm expecting a quick shower and a warm bed."

He couldn't tell if her red cheeks were a result of embarrassment at what she'd just implied or the lights still spinning on top of the emergency vehicles.

"I've got both." He dragged the keys to his bike out of the pocket of his jeans. "I came over here without a helmet, so hold on tight."

He swung one leg over his motorcycle and cranked on the engine. Then he tipped the bike to the side for Scarlett to climb on.

She placed one bare foot on the footrest and hoisted herself on top of the bike behind him.

From his position, he had no idea what she looked like on the back of his bike wearing nothing but a knee-length T-shirt and a motorcycle jacket, but the vision he conjured in his head made him hard.

Twisting his head over his shoulder, he shouted, "Hang on."

Then, as she curled her arms around his waist and pressed her body against his back, he got even harder.

This was gonna be the longest mile of his life.

He aimed his bike down the road, taking it slow, assuring himself it was for safety reasons and not to prolong the sensation of Scarlett wrapped around him, cheek against his back, knees digging into his hips.

He rolled up at his cabin and took the bike around the side. Before he parked it, he leaned it to the left. "Can you get off okay?"

"Yeah."

The leather of his jacket creaked as she peeled herself away from him and then managed a little hop onto the ground. Her T-shirt hiked up, exposing a flash of her shapely thigh.

He parked the motorcycle and jingled the keys in his hand as he walked to the porch of the cabin. "Shower first?"

"Please." She fluffed her hair with her hands. "I smell like smoke."

"Excuse the mess." He pushed open the front door. "I haven't done much cleaning up since I got here."

Folding her arms, she edged into the room, turning her head from side to side. "It's not too bad."

"Yeah, biker chic." He strode to the hallway and plucked a clean towel from the stack in the cupboard. Then he pushed open the bathroom door and hung the towel over the rack. "Do you want a washcloth?"

She came up behind him, framed by the bathroom door. "No, as long as you have some shampoo in there."

"Generic."

"I'm not picky." She tugged at the hem of the still-damp T-shirt.

He made a gun with his fingers, pointing at her. "I can get you a clean T-shirt, maybe a pair of sweats. Anything else of mine you'd be swimming in it."

"A T-shirt's fine."

"Okay, then. I'll leave you to it." They did a little dance as he squeezed past her at the door. She did smell smoky…but still sweet.

He closed the door and as she cranked on the shower, he headed for the bedroom. She'd have to sleep in the bedroom he'd been occupying. The other bedroom still had a bunch of junk in it and no sheets on the bed. At least he'd washed his sheets two days ago.

He'd crash on the couch in the living room. He didn't sleep much, anyway.

His gaze darted around the room, making sure he hadn't left anything embarrassing out in the open. He smoothed a hand over the bedspread and fluffed the pillow as if he was a preparing a hotel bed for a guest.

He pawed through the T-shirts hanging in his closet and grabbed an extra-long black one so she wouldn't suspect him of wanting to see any more of her body—which is exactly what he did want.

He shook out the shirt and placed it on the bed. Leaving the bedroom door open, he grabbed a blanket from the closet and dumped it onto the couch.

"Jim?"

"Yeah?" He looked down the short hall.

She'd poked her towel-wrapped head out of the bathroom door. "Do you have that T-shirt?"

"Comin' right up." He returned to the bedroom and snatched the shirt from the bed. He tapped on the bathroom door. "Got it."

She stuck her hand out the door. "Thanks. Can I use the hair dryer in here?"

"Yeah, of course, if it still works. It was my old man's." He backed up from the door. "You can sleep in the room across the hall. Bed's all ready for you."

The roar of the hair dryer drowned out his words, and he shrugged.

He sat on the edge of the couch and pulled off his boots and then his socks. Had he really been at the sheriff's station tonight suspected of murdering Rusty? It seemed like a hundred years ago.

Why had someone set that fire? And why not set the whole cabin on fire with Scarlett in it? The singed hair on his arms stood up. He had to convince her to go back to San Francisco, even if that meant moving back in with her ex-boyfriend.

He took off his flannel shirt and pulled his T-shirt over his head. He smelled like smoke, too. He yanked off his jeans and tossed everything in a pile near the fireplace.

As he shook out the blanket, Scarlett exclaimed behind him, "Oh, sorry."

He turned, wearing only his boxers, raising his eyebrows. "Do you need something?"

"I wasn't sure where I was supposed to go." She plucked at the neckline of the shirt, which was so baggy it slid off one of her shoulders, dipping to expose the swell of her breast.

What made him think she'd look any less sexy in an oversize T-shirt than a tighter one?

Her gaze wandered over his body, and his flesh prickled with heat.

"I left the bedroom door open for you. The other room isn't habitable."

"I can sleep here on the couch. I don't want to kick you out of your bed."

"Don't worry about it. I've spent a few nights on this couch already." He pointed to the TV in the corner. "Sometimes I just fall asleep in front of the TV."

"Sounds like insomnia to me."

"The least of my current troubles."

She sucked in a breath and reached forward so quickly he couldn't avoid her touch, didn't want to avoid her touch.

Tracing a fingertip over the scar on his chest, she asked, "Is this a souvenir from your captors?"

"One of many."

She flattened her hand against his skin. "I'm sorry. I shouldn't have…"

He swallowed hard, unable to shift his gaze from her plump lips. With a voice rough around the edges, he said, "You don't have to keep being sorry, Scarlett."

"I know." Her long lashes fluttered. "I'll just… Good night."

"Good night."

She spun around and almost ran to the bedroom. When the door clicked shut, Jim let out a long breath.

How the hell was he supposed to let that woman go anywhere?

SCARLETT PRACTICALLY DOVE into the bed. She dragged the pillow against her chest, burying her face in it.

Bad move. The pillowcase had Jim's scent on it—clean, masculine, totally irresistible. She tossed it aside.

When she'd touched the scar on his chest, she hadn't wanted to stop there. She could've run her hands all over his hard body and died a happy woman.

She'd put her momentary lapse in sanity down to smoke inhalation. She didn't need a complicated man like Jim in her life, didn't need to fix him, didn't need to help him solve his problems.

She *could* allow herself one little taste, a little autumn fling. He'd made it pretty clear he wouldn't kick her out of bed or off his couch if she made that move. But who was she kidding?

Flings and shallow affairs were reserved for shallow men—not guys like Jim. If she succumbed to her physical desire for him, she'd be jumping into the deep end without a life jacket.

She rolled to her side, bringing her knees up to her chest, trying not to think about how much warmer she'd be curled up next to Jim. Closing her eyes, she relaxed her muscles and began to drift off.

Minutes or maybe hours later, a crash from the other room had her bolting upright in bed. Had Jim just had another seizure?

Bumps and thumps resounded from the living room, and Scarlett scrambled from the bed. Her gaze darted around the dark room and settled on the shotgun mounted on the wall. She stood on her tiptoes and lifted the gun from its brackets as the cacophony from the other room continued.

Raising the gun to her shoulder, she crept from the bedroom into the living room. Two dark shapes scuffled and scrabbled on the floor, rocking this way and that. Her heart skipped a beat. Someone had broken in and attacked Jim.

She primed the shotgun, pointed the barrel at the ceiling and pulled the trigger. The blast rang in her ears and plaster showered down around her.

The fighting stopped and one of the men staggered to his feet and turned on the light.

Jim, still wearing just his boxers, sporting a trickle of blood beneath his nose, stared at her, and then jerked his head toward the man moaning and sputtering on the floor.

Jim let out a string of curses.

Scarlett turned the gun on the intruder, whose curses had turned into a laugh.

Was he crazy? She leveled the gun at the man's head. "Jim, are you okay? My God, did this man break in?"

"He didn't have to break in. I imagine he still has a key."

"What? You know him?"

"He's my brother."

Chapter Nine

Still cackling, the man sat up and rested his back against the couch. "You still got it, little brother. Always were tougher than me."

Scarlett's mouth dropped open, but she kept the gun trained on Jim's brother.

"What the hell are you doing here, Dax?"

Dax Kennedy wiped a hand across his mouth as his gaze traveled to Scarlett. "You didn't tell me you had a little honey with you, bro."

Jim stepped between her and Dax's gaze. "You can put the gun down, Scarlett."

"Sorry about that." She lowered the shotgun and brushed some plaster from her arm. "But what were you guys rolling around the floor for? I thought someone was going to get killed. I thought Dax was a stranger."

"That's Dax's idea of a joke. He let himself in with his key and jumped me. I didn't know who the hell he was and he didn't bother telling me."

"What would be the fun in that?" Dax pushed up from the floor and adjusted his leather jacket, which sported a patch with the letters *LOC* and a skull with handlebars through it.

"Wanted you to give me your best, J.T." He lifted his chin to look at his taller younger brother. "And your best is pretty damned good."

"What are you doing back here, Dax?" Jim folded his arms and nodded to Scarlett. "Scarlett, you can go back to bed."

"And miss all the drama? No, thanks."

Jim crossed the room in two steps and dragged the blanket from the couch. "You might as well keep warm."

Standing in front of her, he draped the blanket around her shoulders and bunched it together under her chin.

She shuffled to a chair and sat down, curling her legs beneath her, looking from Jim to his brother. Those dark good looks ran in the family, but Dax was a paler, smaller version of Jim—like a poor copy.

"Why are you here and when did you get out of the joint?"

"I've been out for over a year, keeping out of trouble."

Jim tapped the left side of his chest. "You're still riding with the club."

"It's in my blood, bro. I'm an OG now."

"Are you sure you're staying out of trouble?"

Jim bent over to snag his jeans, flashing his back and the tattoo of the motorcycle club he'd escaped. He pulled on his pants.

"The club ain't what it used to be, J.T."

Scarlett asked, "J.T.?"

"My initials, James Thomas, my nickname from the old days." Jim pointed at his brother. "How long have you been here? Did you hear Rusty's dead?"

Dax's head snapped up. "Are you kidding me?"

"Someone offed him two days ago. Stabbed him and left him for dead. Tried to pin it on me."

Dax's dark eyes narrowed and he stroked his goatee. "You're serious."

"I'm serious. The killer used one of Slick's hunting knives—stole it from the garage."

"The SOB didn't touch the bikes, did he?"

"Didn't touch the bikes." Jim hooked his thumbs in his front pockets, and his unbuttoned jeans dipped lower. "And I saw Chewy in town. What is this, some kinda Lords reunion?"

"Chewy, huh?" Dax pushed his long hair out of his face. "Are you going to introduce me to your friend, or just stand here and give me the third degree?"

"This is Scarlett Easton. Scarlett, my brother, Dax Kennedy."

Scarlett poked her hand from the blanket and waved.

"Scarlett? You're that pretty little Indian girl from J.T.'s class."

Jim rolled his eyes.

Scarlett stuck two fingers behind her head and wiggled them. "That's me…the little Indian girl."

Dax threw back his head and barked out a laugh. "I like you. I like her, J.T. She your woman?"

She wished.

"I live up the road, and someone set fire to the trees around my property tonight. You wouldn't know anything about that, would you?"

"Me? What the hell has this guy been telling you about his older brother? Why would I want to set fire to your place? And what the hell is going on around here? Murders, fires, setups."

Jim folded his arms and widened his stance. "You never answered my question. What brings you back to Timberline?"

"You. Heard you were back."

"Who told you that?"

"Does it matter? Thought we could settle some of the old man's stuff." He held up his hands. "You can have the cabin, but I might want a couple of those bikes."

"I don't have a problem with that. You plan to stay here? In this cabin?"

"Bro, I've been riding all night. I need a place to crash."

Scarlett hopped up from the chair. "Dax, you

take the couch. Jim, you can have your bed back. I mean, uh, share it with me."

Winking, Dax slapped Jim on the back. "Sounds like a good deal for you, J.T."

Jim shot her a glance. "I don't want… If you…"

"I'm fine with it." She shrugged out of the blanket and dropped it back on the couch. "Now I really need to get a few hours of sleep."

She left the two brothers talking in low voices and crawled beneath the covers, keeping to one side of the king-size bed. When life gave you lemons, make the whole dang lemon meringue pie and stuff your face.

Jim tapped on the door. "Scarlett?"

"C'mon in."

He slipped into the room and clicked the door behind him. "Are you sure you're okay with this?"

"Your brother's a pretty rough character. Honestly, I figured I'd feel safer with you in here, anyway."

"Dax? Yeah, he has his issues, but harassing women isn't one of them." Jim sat on the edge of the bed and fell back onto his side, his feet still planted on the floor.

"Whoa, mister." She placed her hands on his back and gave him a shove.

"Change your mind already?"

"You're not climbing into this bed wearing those jeans. They still smell like smoke."

He got off the bed and, with his back turned to her, he yanked off his pants. He turned back the covers and slipped in beside her. "Good night, Scarlett."

Poking his shoulder, she asked, "Are you going to find out what Dax is doing here? He didn't exactly give you a straight answer."

"Dax isn't too good at straight answers, but I'll get it out of him—one way or another. Good night."

She turned her back to him and closed her eyes with a smile on her face. His body heat was warming up the bed already. The two of them could warm it up a lot faster, but his brother in the next room was saving her from making a big mistake.

Or keeping her from the time of her life.

THE NEXT MORNING, Scarlett peeled open one eye and followed a shaft of light beaming through a hitch in the blinds. She rolled toward Jim's now-empty side of the bed and inhaled the scent he'd left behind—slightly smoky and woodsy.

Another smell floated through the air, replacing it. This one made her mouth water almost as much as the other—and she didn't even eat bacon.

She scooted out of the bed and landed in front of Jim's closet, where a row of T-shirts swayed on their hangers. She pulled another black T from the bunch and swapped it with the huge one Jim had picked out for her last night. Had he given her that one just so that it would fall off her?

A girl could hope.

"Hello?" She poked her head into the hallway. "Everyone decent?"

Dax yelled back. "I'm never decent, sweetheart."

She tiptoed into the living room and raised her brows at Dax in the kitchen, spatula in one hand and oven mitt on the other. "You cook?"

"Nothing fancy. Went to the store and picked up some eggs and bacon, potatoes, bread." He waved the spatula at the counter. "Dig in."

"Where's Jim?" She hunched over the counter and picked up a piece of toast.

"In the shower, I think."

Scarlett bit into the toast and dropped it on a plate. She scooped some scrambled eggs onto her dish and added some potatoes. After several bites, she said, "Not bad. Where'd you learn how to cook?"

"From my mom. She taught me a few things before she ran off, and then I cooked for my dad and brother when she did. J.T. was just a little guy when Wendy, our mom abandoned us— maybe four, and I was thirteen."

She wrinkled her nose as she did the calculations in her head. Jim's mom must've left right before the kidnappings. When Jim had told his story of almost being snatched from his bed, he hadn't mentioned his mother. She must've been gone by then.

"You really stepped up." She crunched into her toast, her assessment of Dax Kennedy shifting by the minute.

"I thought you were a vegetarian." Jim came up behind her, toweling off his dark hair, the muscles across his chest and shoulders bunching and flexing.

"I eat eggs." She held up a forkful of scrambled egg.

"Yeah, but these potatoes?" He snatched one from her plate. "Cooked in bacon grease."

"Oh." She shoved the potatoes to the side of her plate. "Thanks for warning me."

"You didn't have to cook breakfast, Dax." Jim took a plate from the stack and loaded it with everything.

"I figured I wouldn't get anything to eat if I left it up to you, unless you learned how to cook in the army." He jerked his thumb at Jim. "This guy never stepped one foot in the kitchen."

"Are you going to tell me what you're doing in Timberline?"

Dax paused, a piece of bacon dangling from a pair of tongs over the sizzling frying pan. He dropped the bacon onto a plate covered with a paper towel. "Thought I told you, bro. Wanted to check out the old man's place."

Jim grunted and then dug into his food.

Scarlett planted her elbows on the counter. "Do you mind if I ask you a question, Dax?"

"Shoot."

"What were you in prison for?"

"A few things. I don't even remember anymore."

Jim raised his fork in the air. "Try armed robbery, possession of narcotics with the intent to sell."

"Oh, yeah. Never intended to use that gun."

"Because you led such a peaceful existence otherwise."

Dax ducked his head in the fridge. "Motorcycle club business."

"Doesn't excuse it."

"Okay, sorry I asked. I didn't mean to stir up trouble." Scarlett aimed her fork at Jim. "Have the investigators from the fire department been around yet?"

"No." Jim glanced at his brother. "Have they?"

"I wasn't up much earlier than you, but I didn't hear anything."

Scarlett plucked at the T-shirt. "I'd really like to get back into my place and at least pick up some clothes if they won't let me stay there."

"I think they'll let you back in." Jim broke a piece of bacon in two and popped one half in his mouth. "The fire didn't reach the cabin. The fire department may have soaked your roof and if you had any leaks, you might be in trouble, but I didn't see any damage to your cabin."

"It's been raining on and off since I've been back. I know I don't have any leaks." She spread her arms. "Not like the Kennedy brothers haven't offered me first-class hospitality."

Dax chuckled and then whistled an unidentifiable tune as he piled his plate with food. He brought it to the small kitchen table, stationed near a sliding door that led to a small patio decorated with a rusted barbecue and a dead plant.

"If Scarlett's going back to her place, can I bunk here, J.T.?"

"Are you into anything illegal? Weapons? Drugs? Pimping?"

Scarlett swallowed her orange juice the wrong way and coughed. Her rising opinion of Dax had just taken a nosedive.

"Hey, hey." Dax leveled his fork at Jim. "I never ran the girls."

"Whatever. If you're running anything, hit the road. You can't stay here."

"Scout's honor." Dax held up two fingers. "I'm clean. Even gave up the drugs and booze."

"You're kidding."

"I gave up the drugs and the hard drinking. I can handle a beer or two. I got a woman in Seattle now. Belinda won't put up with that stuff."

A knock on the door interrupted their conversation, and Jim strode to the door. He peered through the peephole. "Looks like the arson investigators."

He opened the door to two men in suits, and Scarlett tugged her T-shirt below her knees.

How much more uncomfortable could this get?

Jim shook hands with them and invited them inside. "This is Scarlett Easton. The fire was at her place. Scarlett, this is Investigator Young and Investigator Elgin."

"Excuse me for not getting up, but I ran outside in my pajamas last night and all my clothes are at my house."

"We just have a few questions, Ms. Easton."

Jim gestured toward Dax, still stuffing his face. "This is my brother and he was just leaving."

Jim grabbed a key chain from a hook in the kitchen and tossed it to Dax. "Have a look at those bikes in the garage. Let me know what you want to keep and what we can sell, and be on the lookout for the cops. They're coming to dust for prints around the garage—had a break-in earlier."

"Great, cops." Dax stacked up all their dishes and dumped them into the sink. "I'm outta here."

Scarlett stayed where she was at the counter, while Jim sat at the kitchen table with the two investigators.

They asked questions about any noises she may have heard—none—and any other unusual activity around her place.

"You mean like a dead body in the woods?"

Neither Young nor Elgin batted an eyelash. They must've already been briefed about Rusty Kelly.

Jim asked, "Did you confirm it was arson?"

"Preliminary findings point to arson. We discovered some accelerant at the base of several trees in different areas."

Scarlett rubbed the goose bumps from her arms, even though the findings didn't surprise her. Did someone want to kill her or just drive her away? And why?

Jim shot her a glance and asked, "Can you track down who did it? Will it be easy?"

"Depends on what else we discover. If this is a serial arsonist, he'll probably strike again."

Scarlett exchanged another glance with Jim. They both knew this was no serial arsonist. She'd been targeted.

"When can Ms. Easton go home?"

"You can go home now, Ms. Easton. Just stay out of the areas cordoned off with yellow tape. We'll be sifting through the remains. When we're done, you can clean the place."

She blew out a breath. "There goes my privacy."

"I can't say that bothers me much." Jim pushed

away from the table and joined her at the counter, squeezing her hand. "You're too isolated back there. Maybe it'll even improve your cell reception."

The investigators stood up. "That's all we have for now. If we discover anything else or need to ask you any more questions, we'll contact you."

Jim walked them to the door. When he shut it behind them, he turned and said, "You wanna go home?"

"Yes, it would be nice to put some pants on. And shoes—shoes would be good."

"You want to put on a pair of my sweatpants for the ride back?"

"Absolutely. That Lady Godiva stuff is okay for the wee hours of the morning, but I could get arrested for that this time of day."

He quirked an eyebrow at her, and she could feel a surge of warmth in her cheeks. She'd never blushed so much in her entire life than she had these past few days with Jim—must be her heightened sense of awareness…or how he looked in a pair of jeans.

"I have a clean pair of sweats in the bottom drawer of the dresser in the bedroom."

"I'll find them." She made for the bedroom and crouched in front of the dresser, pulling open the last drawer. She plunged her hands into the soft material and her fingers stumbled across some hard, metal objects.

She parted the sweats and sweatshirts and closed her hand around one of the objects, pulling it out of the drawer. She held it up, the dull gold of the medal glinting in the light.

She ran her thumb along the raised lettering on the disc. It was some kind of medal for bravery. She peered into the drawer at the other medals. If he wore every one of them at once, he'd be bowed over from the weight.

These couldn't all be recognition for surviving and escaping his capture. He'd been a sniper. He must've gotten medals for killing people— lots of people.

His imprisonment and torture must've gone a long way toward alleviating any guilt he'd felt about that. She stuffed the medals back into the drawer. Somehow she didn't think Jim would feel guilty about doing his job, about killing the enemy and saving his brothers in arms.

"You ready?"

"Just about." She snatched up a pair of dark blue sweats and pulled them on. She pushed up the elastic to her calves and cinched the waist as much as she could.

"Ready." She stepped into the hallway and Jim met her with a helmet.

"I do have this for you."

She took it from him, tucking it under her arm. As they walked out the front door, Dax revved the engine of a Harley parked next to Jim's.

"This one's a beauty. Mind if I keep it for myself?"

"Take what you like, Dax, but leave a couple since I promised Scarlett's cousin he could buy one."

Jim flipped up the kickstand on his bike and mounted it. He dipped it to one side. "Hop on."

With a lot more confidence than this morning, Scarlett hitched one leg over the seat of the bike and settled behind Jim. She even leaned against the backrest, hooking her fingers in Jim's belt loops, but when he started the bike and rolled onto the road, she grabbed him around the waist.

When he pulled up in front of her mailbox, she dug her fingers into his side. Her cabin stood in the center of a ring of blackened and charred trees and foliage. Soggy, yellow tape stirred in the breeze, waving a sorry welcome.

Jim steered his bike up to her front porch and cut the engine. "Looks like a war zone."

She lifted the helmet from her head and shook out her hair. "There goes my little hideaway. The cabin is completely visible from the road now."

"You can replant, but give yourself a clear view of the road this time."

"I hope everything doesn't smell like smoke in there." She slid from the bike.

"You'll probably have to air it out and clean up."

She jogged up the two steps to the front door and tried the handle. "Great. It's unlocked."

She pushed open the front door and hovered on the threshold, sniffing the air. "It doesn't smell too bad and I don't see any damage from the fire hoses or flame retardant."

"You should check your studio. You're probably going to have to clean all those windows in there."

Jim left the door open, and she edged down the hallway toward the studio. The door had been left open. Had the firefighters come inside her place? She never left that door open.

Pushing the door back, she scanned the room. Her current canvas was in place and undamaged, but Jim had been right. Streaks of flame retardant and rivulets of water clouded the glass walls of the studio, practically blocking the view to the outside world.

"I'm going to have to get a professional window cleaner in here to take care of this mess, unless my cousin Annie can do it."

"Add a professional landscaper to clean up the mess outside."

Scarlett wandered around the room, unease tickling the back of her neck. She flipped through some canvases and took a step back to scan one wall covered with her landscape paintings.

"What's wrong?"

"I'm not sure. Something feels off."

"Something missing? You do have an inventory, don't you?"

She tapped her head. "The inventory is up here."

"And?"

"Can't put my finger on it yet."

"Make sure you check all your stuff, and if there's anything missing, make a report."

Scarlett paused in front of an easel with her current project clipped onto it, the smell of paint tickling her nose. Glancing at the tray, she noticed a pot of open black paint and a dirty brush.

Her pulse thrummed in her throat as she ran a fingertip across the damp ends of the brush. "This is weird."

"What?" Jim joined her at the easel.

"There's an open pot of paint and a used brush. I always clean up when I'm done."

"You mean someone broke into your place, came in here and painted a picture?" He scratched his head.

She dabbed her fingers across the painting on the easel. "Maybe someone just wanted to be helpful and finish this work for me."

She barked out a short, dry laugh and licked

her lips. She turned toward the wall of paintings again, her gaze scanning each row.

"Does the second row from the bottom look crooked to you?"

Jim squeezed past her, and his head swung from side to side. "Yeah, it's this bunch here on the right."

He shuffled to the right and reached up to adjust the frames on the wall. "Scarlett!"

She jumped at the sharpness of his tone. "What's wrong?"

"You might want to have a look at this forest painting."

She tripped forward, grabbing onto Jim's arm as she leaned toward the painting.

She gasped, her fingers digging into his biceps. Someone had altered one of her landscapes—adding three stick figures at the edge of the forest, holding hands.

Chapter Ten

A chill snaked down Scarlett's spine, and she took a step back, dropping her hold on Jim.

Jim leaned in for a closer look. "You know what that's supposed to be, don't you?"

Scarlett swore and pushed past him. She grabbed the painting from the wall. "Some crude representation of the Timberline Trio. It's sick. Who would do this?"

"Put the frame down and don't touch the paintbrush or paint."

She dropped the painting on the floor. "You really think the sheriff's department is going to come out here and fingerprint over what amounts to a bad paint job?"

"When we tell them what was painted, they will. They're investigating this fire as arson. They'll be interested."

She flicked her fingers at the painting. "What

do you think it means? Who is it that won't let this case die?"

"Maybe it's a warning to do just that—let it die. There's been a lot of attention focused on the case these past few months. The kidnapper or kidnappers were never caught and the children never found—dead or alive. This spotlight on the case must be making someone nervous."

"I get that, but why me? I haven't opened an investigation into the Timberline Trio. And what does it all have to do with Rusty?"

"Or my brother."

"So you don't believe he's here looking at your dad's bikes?"

"Too coincidental—him, Rusty, Chewy. What are they all doing here at the same time?"

"A biker reunion?"

"Right." He put his hand on the small of her back and steered her out of the studio. "Let's go outside and call the police to report this."

A deputy came out faster than Scarlett expected but found only one set of prints on the paint and the frame, which had to be hers.

The deputy took it more seriously because of the fire, but he didn't know what to make of it any more than she and Jim did. He took pictures and notes, but there wasn't much else he could do.

When he left, Scarlett collapsed in a chair and crossed her arms behind her head. "I don't get it.

What do I have to do with the Timberline Trio? I was just a kid when it happened."

"Have you ever questioned your granny or any of the elders about why they wouldn't discuss the case?"

"They shut me down every time I tried."

He nodded toward the studio. "Maybe it's time to try again now that you're involved."

"I never did drop off that yarn I picked up for Granny." She pushed out of the chair. "How about it? Feel like a trip to the reservation?"

"Don't think I'm welcome."

"The Quileute had an issue with your dad and Dax, never you."

"Guilt by association."

"Well, you'll be with me."

Jim glanced at his watch. "What time are we taking this field trip?"

"Do you mind?"

"No. I want to know as much as you do, but I want to talk to Dax, too."

"Do you think you can get him to admit what he's really doing here?"

"Nobody can get Dax to do anything he doesn't want to do—the only one who could was the old man and he used threats of violence."

"Okay, you talk to Dax." She held up her dead cell phone. "I'm going to charge up my phone and call a few landscapers. I'm also going to buy a landline phone and hook up my service."

"Good idea." He hesitated by the front door. "Are you going to be okay here by yourself?"

"I'll be fine. Besides, my cabin is fully visible from the road now."

"That's not a bad thing, Scarlett." He raised his hand and slipped out the door.

WHEN JIM PULLED up to his cabin, Dax looked up from tinkering with a motorcycle and wiped his hands on a rag hanging over the handlebars of the bike.

Jim parked his Harley and joined his brother. "You need any help?"

"You can hand me that wrench by your right foot."

Crouching down, Jim swept up the tool and handed it to Dax.

"Took you long enough to get back. Did you and that feisty chick finally get it on?" Dax loosened a spark plug with the wrench.

"No, and if we had, I wouldn't be telling you about it. Someone broke into Scarlett's place and defaced one of her paintings."

"That sucks. You think it's the same person who set the fire?" Dax squinted at the spark plug he was trying to remove.

"Probably. You know what the person put on her painting?"

"Something obscene?"

"Kind of. Someone painted three stick figures at the edge of a forest scene, holding hands."

Dax dropped the wrench and swore. "What's that supposed to mean?"

"It's obviously the Timberline Trio."

"Obviously? How'd you get that out of three stick figures?"

"Holding hands?"

"Maybe it's supposed to be like a threesome or something—I told you, something obscene, although…"

Jim kicked his brother's booted foot. "It wasn't supposed to be a threesome, Dax. It was a representation of the Timberline Trio."

"Bro, you're obsessed with that case." Dax threw his ponytail over his shoulder.

"You know why I am." Jim picked up the wrench and tossed it from hand to hand. "What do you know about that night? The night someone tried to abduct me?"

"I don't know nothin', J.T. I was sleeping, remember?"

"What are you doing in Timberline, Dax?" Jim rose to his feet and crossed his arms over his chest as he loomed over his brother.

"This is gettin' old. If you don't want me to have any of Slick's bikes, just say so."

"It's not about the…forget it." Jim dropped the wrench onto the ground and went to the house.

Dax had tried to cover it, but he'd been rattled when Jim told him about the stick figures. Why?

The sudden appearance of Rusty, Chewy and Dax meant something, and Jim had a sick feeling that their presence in Timberline was related to the fire at Scarlett's.

Jim cleaned up the rest of the breakfast dishes and went into the bedroom for his laundry basket. He fingered the T-shirt Scarlett had folded on top of his bed and then pressed it to his face.

The sweet, clean scent triggered all kinds of memories of the early morning hours he'd spent with her. He tossed the shirt into the basket. He couldn't believe he'd had that woman in his bed, right beside him and had been able to resist her.

Not that falling asleep next to her warm, soft body had been easy. He'd felt every breath from her parted lips, every shift in movement, every touch as her hand or leg brushed against his body.

It had been torture.

He threw his laundry in the washer and wandered back outside to help his brother, who eyed him with suspicion.

Jim held up his hands. "No more questions. I'm just here to help you."

The brothers worked side by side for over an hour until a call from Scarlett came through on

Jim's cell phone. He wiped his hands on the rag and answered the call.

"What's up, Scarlett?" He ignored Dax's raised eyebrows.

"I'm picking up a phone today and my service should be turned on by tomorrow. I also got two estimates from a couple of landscapers, and I'm going with the one my cousin Jason knows. Are you ready?"

"I've been helping Dax work on a bike. I need to shower and change. Do you want to go over on my motorcycle?"

"Sure. My car is filthy from the fire."

"I'll be kind of conspicuous on the bike. Are you sure you don't want to keep my visit a secret?"

"Kind of hard to keep a guy your size a secret."

"Let's just try not to draw attention to ourselves. Nobody needs to know why we're there."

"I have every right to visit Granny and bring an old high school friend. Is a half an hour enough time for you?"

"Sure. Tell you what. You bring your dirty car over here and I'll have Dax wash it for you."

"If you think he won't mind."

Jim watched his brother through narrowed eyes. "He likes anything having to do with cars. Bring it over."

Scarlett ended the call, and Jim tucked his phone into his front pocket.

"Hot date?" Dax pushed a lock of hair from his forehead with a dirty thumb, leaving a smudge of grease.

"We're going to the reservation."

Dax narrowed his eyes. "What for?"

"Scarlett is going to drop off something for her grandmother."

"And she needs your help, why?"

"She just wants the company." If Dax could be closemouthed about his motivations, so could he. He'd told his brother plenty and had gotten nothing in return. "You mind washing her car if she leaves it here?"

"No problem."

By the time Jim had showered and changed, Scarlett had pulled up to the cabin. He charged outside before she could get into conversation with Dax. He didn't want her telling his brother about their mission.

As she greeted Dax, Jim tried to catch her eye, but she ignored him.

"Is that one of the bikes you're going to take?"

Dax stood up, shoving the rag in his back pocket. "If I can get it running. Why are you taking my brother to the rez?"

"My grandmother wanted to meet him after I told her he rescued me from the fire."

Jim let out a measured breath. He didn't have to worry about Scarlett.

"Yeah, that's our J.T." Dax pounded Jim on the back. "Hero material."

"I hope you're not being sarcastic, because he really was heroic when he barged through that fire to get to me."

"I totally mean it. He was always the good brother—" Dax quirked his eyebrows up and down "—and I was the bad boy."

"You didn't have to be, Dax. You let Slick influence you too much."

He squeezed the back of Jim's neck in a vise. "Some of us are just born that way."

"We'd better get going." Jim shrugged him off.

"Are you sure you're okay with washing my car?"

"It'll be the best damned car wash you ever had." Dax winked. "Have fun, you two."

Jim wheeled his bike toward the road, away from Dax. He handed her the helmet and swung his leg over the bike, straddling it.

As Scarlett pulled the helmet on her head, she asked, "Did you get anything out of him today?"

"Nope. That's why I'm glad you didn't say anything to him about why we were going to see your grandmother." Jim started the engine of the Harley. "If he's not going to be straight with me, I'm not going to be straight with him—not until I know what he's doing here."

"I agree. Did you tell him about the painting?"

"Yeah, and it rattled him, as much as anything can rattle Dax."

"But he didn't say anything about it?"

"He made jokes about it."

She puffed out a breath. "Has Dax seen the other guy, yet? Chewy?"

"I don't think so, but I don't expect him to tell me about it."

Scarlett climbed onto the bike behind him, and her arms around his waist gave him a thrill like he hadn't felt for a woman in a long time.

He liked Scarlett. He'd always liked her, even way back in high school. She'd been different from the other teenage girls—always had a purpose. But just because their attraction seemed mutual, it didn't mean he had to act on that attraction. He wasn't ready for a relationship, and Scarlett wasn't the type of woman you loved and left.

He drove north to the Quileute reservation, following a road that meandered next to a river, bordered by lush forest on either side. The reservation came into view, the small houses dotting the landscape, the roadside vendors selling their wares.

When his bike came into view of an old woman and a young girl on the side of the road, the girl jumped up and down and waved. Jim held up his hand.

Slowing down, he steered his motorcycle onto

the Quileute land until Scarlett tapped his arm. He pulled up to a small, brown-and-green house.

When he cut the engine, Scarlett said, "Thanks for waving to Prudence back there. You probably made her day."

"Prudence? The girl with the old woman?"

Scarlett took off the helmet and handed it to him. "She goes to the reservation school but wants to transfer to the public school next year. I'm trying to make that happen by convincing her grandmother that Pru will blossom in the public school environment."

"You did."

She jerked her head to the side and her hair fell over one eye. "I don't know about that. It did introduce me to Mrs. Rooney, my art teacher, and she's the one who encouraged me to go to art school instead of regular college."

He nodded. "Blossomed."

A little smile lifted one corner of her mouth as she pointed to the low-slung brown-and-green house that looked like it grew up out of the forest. "Granny really does want to meet you. I wasn't lying to Dax about that."

"You told her about me?"

"Of course. I told her the whole story about finding the body and the fire."

"Did you tell her about the stick figures?"

"No. I'd rather see her reaction."

He got off the bike and planted one booted

foot on the ground, cranking his head to the side. "Nobody's going to come after me with pitchforks, are they?"

"At least you didn't say tomahawks." She nudged his shoulder. "What are you so worried about? Nobody remembers what a bigot your dad was."

"And Dax. Don't forget him."

"He seems to have reformed and mellowed. Besides, Granny always was one to make her own judgments of people."

"My kind of woman."

She squeezed his biceps. "You're her kind of man, too. Don't let her sexually harass you."

Jim laughed, but Scarlett just raised her eyebrows before turning and striding toward her granny's house. She tapped on the front door and called out, "Granny?"

A strong voice answered. "I'm here, Scarlett."

Jim followed Scarlett into the house, already warmed by a blaze in the fireplace. Scarlett's grandmother waved them over. "C'mon over here. I don't bite, but I might make an exception in your case."

As she laughed, her thin shoulders shook.

"Granny, behave yourself or you're going to scare off Jim."

The old woman gripped the arms of her chair and sized him up through large, dark eyes that took up half her face. "He doesn't look like a man who scares easily."

"Yeah, well, he's never met someone like you before." Scarlett crossed the small room and dipped down to kiss her grandmother's cheek. "Granny, this is Jim Kennedy. Jim, my grandmother."

Jim joined Scarlett and took her grandmother's thin hand in his. "Nice to meet you, ma'am."

"Nice to meet you, too, young man and you can call me Evelyn. Granny this, granny that—makes me feel ancient."

"I brought you the yarn." Scarlett waved it in the air.

"Drop it in the basket. Would you two like something to drink? Tea? Coffee?" Evelyn winked. "Something a little stronger?"

"Jim doesn't drink, Granny, and it's a little early for me."

"Nothing like Slick, are you?"

"No, ma'am, and some water would be fine."

"Go make us some tea, Scarlett, and bring Jim a glass of water."

"Okay." Scarlett rolled her eyes at him before she headed for the kitchen.

Evelyn patted the cushion beside her. "Have a seat, Jim."

He sat down, turning his body slightly to face her and her penetrating stare.

"War hero, huh?"

"I just survived is all."

"Did you?" She curved her bony fingers around his wrist with surprising strength and closed her eyes. Her frail body bolted upright and her eyelashes fluttered.

"You did more than survive. You helped the others, but—" she squeezed harder "—you have guilt. So much guilt. They took the other three but left you."

"The other three?" Jim licked his lips. She couldn't be talking about the cell in Afghanistan anymore. He'd been held there with more than three people.

"Do you mean the Timberline Trio?"

Evelyn's eyes flew open. "Is that why you're here?"

"Granny, are you reading him?" Scarlett walked into the room with a tray in front of her.

Evelyn released his wrist. "Why are you back in Timberline, Jim?"

"Going through my father's things."

Evelyn narrowed her eyes as she took her cup from Scarlett. "Don't try to fool an old woman, Jim."

"Especially an old woman who has the gift." Scarlett sat down next to him and put his water and her tea on the table in front of them. "Why don't you tell Granny what happened to you as a child?"

"I thought—" Jim pinged the water glass with his fingernail "—that topic was off-limits here."

Evelyn's dark eyes focused on Scarlett over the rim of her cup. "Is that what you told him?"

"Come on, Granny. How many times did you tell me to stop asking questions about the kidnappings? How many times was I shushed by the elders?"

Evelyn lifted her narrow shoulders. "Most of those elders are dead."

"You mean you're ready to talk now?" Scarlett hunched forward, her thigh bumping his.

"I don't know what you imagine I know, Scarlett, but I want to hear from Jim first. What happened to you? You still carry it with you even after everything else you went through during the war, your captivity."

"My cap— How did you know about that?"

"I felt it, Jim. Tell me what happened in Timberline."

He launched into the story about his attempted kidnapping and how his father had threatened him with bodily harm if he dared tell another soul about it.

Evelyn listened with her eyes closed and through occasional sips of tea, nodding calmly as if his story didn't surprise her one bit.

When he finished, the silence hung heavy over the room, and Evelyn appeared to be sleeping.

Jim raised his brows at Scarlett, who put a finger against her lips.

Evelyn drew in a breath and inhaled the steam from her hot tea. "You probably believe there was bad blood between the Quileute and the Lords of Chaos, don't you do?"

"I know my father for what he was—a bigot. He held ugly stereotypes about the Quileute and wasn't shy about voicing them."

"There was that side of him. Do you think our tribe was completely blameless?"

"I know there were fights."

"There were fights. We had our own trouble-makers. Did you know that?"

"Young men with not a lot to do?" Jim swirled the water in his glass. He'd been one of those. "I can believe that."

"They managed to keep busy with…other activities—illegal activities."

"Are you telling me that the Lords of Chaos and the Quileute were working together?"

"They had business that crossed paths."

"Granny, what does this all have to do with the Timberline Trio?"

"Drugs." Jim placed his glass on the table with a click. "The Lords of Chaos moved drugs through the Washington peninsula and they got them from suppliers."

"Some of our tribe members were suppliers

of drugs?" Scarlett's gaze darted between him and Evelyn.

He'd let Evelyn give her the bad news.

The old woman dropped her chin to her chest. "They were bad apples, Scarlett. Even as a child you must've been aware of your uncle Danny and his feud with your father. Of course, Danny's influence never spread to the entire tribe, despite his best efforts."

"But the elders must've known about it, known about Danny." Scarlett jumped up from the sofa and took a turn around the room, her arms folded across her chest. "Why else would they try to protect these *bad apples*?"

"Nothing was known for sure. There was no proof."

"Wait, wait, wait." Scarlett pressed two fingers against her temple. "I still don't understand what this all has to do with the Timberline Trio kidnappings."

Evelyn laced her fingers together in her lap. "I can't tell you that. I only know the Lords of Chaos and that gang of Quileute were in business together, and I believe that business involved the kidnapping of those children. Now that I've heard Jim's story, I'm more convinced than ever."

Jim ran his knuckles across his jaw. "Did the elders tell you to keep quiet, Evelyn?"

"They did." She held up her hand at Scarlett, who had begun to speak. "I didn't have any proof

I could take to the police, anyway, Scarlett, so don't give me that look. I was never allowed to get that proof."

"Was there any evidence?" Scarlett sat on the edge of the coffee table and clasped her grandmother's hand.

"There was the pink ribbon."

"Pink ribbon?" Jim and Scarlett said the words in unison.

"You found it. Don't you remember, Scarlett? You picked it up off the ground. You brought it to me and complained that it felt hot in your hands. You didn't understand your gift yet, so you didn't realize what the ribbon's warmth meant."

Jim interrupted her. "But you did."

"I couldn't get a read on it." Evelyn wrapped her hands around her cup as if to warm them. "And then it was stolen from me."

"I stole it."

The cup in Evelyn's hands jerked, sloshing the tea inside. "You took the ribbon?"

"I couldn't understand why you wouldn't let me keep the ribbon, so I snuck into your knitting basket and took it back."

"How do you know this—" Jim twirled his finger in the air "—pink ribbon had something to do with the Timberline Trio case?"

Evelyn wrinkled her nose and screwed up her eyes as if looking into the past. "I didn't at first. I just wanted to protect Scarlett from any visions she wouldn't know how to handle. But then the gossip started up about the kidnappings. I'd heard from someone who'd heard from someone else that a pink ribbon was taken from one of the little kidnapped girls—Kayla Rush. When I heard that, I went to retrieve the ribbon, but someone had taken it."

Scarlett raised her hand. "That would be me."

"I suppose it's too much to hope for that you still have it somewhere." Jim blew out a breath.

"Yeah. I mean, I have some trinkets and mementos from my childhood, but I can't imagine I still have a ribbon."

"You never showed it to anyone, did you?" Evelyn struggled to sit forward, and Jim reached over the table to take her hand.

"Maybe a few friends. I don't remember." Scarlett dipped next to the table and gathered Jim's glass and her own mug. "Do you think that's why I'm involved now? Somebody thinks I know something?"

"Perhaps." Evelyn reached for her knitting in the basket at her feet. "A few of that bunch have returned to the reservation recently, including Danny."

"That's interesting." Jim moved the basket within Evelyn's reach. "A few of the Lords of Chaos have returned to Timberline, too. Is someone or something calling them home?"

Evelyn's hand trembled slightly as she picked up her needles. "I hope not."

"We'll get out of your hair, Granny. If you think of anything else, let us know." Scarlett stroked her grandmother's head.

"Thanks, Evelyn."

She aimed one of her knitting needles at Jim. "You have nothing to feel guilty about, young man."

He winked at her and followed Scarlett from the house. "That was enlightening but not useful."

"Oh, I don't know. I could look for that pink ribbon and try to get something out of it."

"That's a long shot." As he approached his bike parked outside Evelyn's house, his spine stiffened and then he cursed.

"What's wrong?"

Jim strode to his bike and dropped to his knees. "Someone slashed my tires."

Chapter Eleven

Goose bumps raced up Scarlett's arms, and she jerked her head to the side to scan the road. Was this malicious mischief because someone didn't want Jim Kennedy here or was it because someone didn't want them talking to Granny about the Timberline Trio?

"I'm pretty sure someone did this with a knife." Jim ran his hands along the shredded pieces of his tire.

Crouching beside Jim, her shoulder bumping his, she asked, "Who would do something like this here?"

"Either it's someone on the reservation with an old grudge against Slick or someone with a new grudge against me."

A truck rolled up, spewing exhaust, and Scarlett rose to her feet and covered her nose and mouth with one hand.

Her cousin Jason waved through the window.

He parked next to Jim's bike and hopped out of his truck. "I thought it was my turn to look in on Granny."

"I had something to drop off."

Jason's eyes widened as he took in Jim examining his bike's tires. "What happened?"

Jim cranked his head around. "I guess someone wanted to keep me on the reservation."

"Someone here did that?" Jason scratched his head beneath his black beanie.

"Did you just get here? Did you see anything?" Scarlett studied her cousin's face.

"Me?" He stabbed his chest with his thumb. "You think I did this?"

"Did I say that? I just asked if you saw anything...or anyone."

Jason took a step back toward his truck. "I just drove onto the rez. I didn't see anyone running away or burning rubber or anything like that if that's what you mean."

Jim brushed his hands together and pushed to his feet. "Resentment of the Lords still run high around here?"

"Not that I know of. That was a long time ago, man. This isn't going to hurt my chances of buying one of those sweet bikes, is it?"

"Not if you give your cousin, me and my bike a ride back to my place."

"Yeah, sure. No problem." He pointed to Granny's house. "Should I stop in to see her?"

"I'm sure she'll want to see you, but—" Scarlett grabbed Jason's arm as he started to move toward the house "—don't tell her what happened out here. I don't want her to worry."

"Whatever, but I don't think Granny's going to be worried about Jim's tires getting slashed."

"Just keep it to yourself. Shh."

"Okay if I load my bike into your truck bed?"

"Go ahead, or you can wait for me and I'll help you." Jason continued up the steps and disappeared inside the house.

"Do you think he knows anything?" Jim lowered the back of Jason's truck and shoved a hand in his pocket as he scoured the landscape through narrowed eyes.

"No. What are you looking for?"

"Something I can use as a ramp."

"Granny has some old construction materials in the back of her house. I keep telling her to toss the stuff, but she hates to throw anything away."

"Lead the way."

She crooked her finger, and Jim followed her around the side of the house. "Wood?"

"That'll work."

Together, they hauled a two-by-four to the front of the house. Jim wedged it against the back of Jason's truck just as Jason exited the house.

"I can help you with that." He jogged over and took Scarlett's place on the other side of the ramp. "I'll secure it while you roll the bike up."

Jim wheeled his bike up the makeshift ramp and put it on its side. "I appreciate it."

She asked her cousin, "You didn't mention this to Granny, did you?"

"Said Jim was having problems with his bike and I was giving you two a ride back."

"Thanks." She hopped into the truck after Jason and Jim squeezed in beside her.

On the ride back to Timberline, the three of them discussed who could be behind the vandalism of Jim's bike, but she and Jim kept mum about their true suspicions.

When they arrived at Jim's cabin, he and Jason unloaded the bike, and Jim invited him into the garage to look at the other motorcycles.

While Jim and Jason were in the garage, Scarlett sat on Jim's front porch, stretching her legs in front of her and tapping the toes of her boots together. Dax and his bike were gone, but she figured he'd be back. He had business in Timberline, and Jim was convinced that business involved more than looking over Slick's motorcycles.

Jason emerged from the garage with a big smile on his face.

She called out, "You see something you like?"

"Oh, yeah. Do you want a ride back to your cabin? I drove by earlier and it's still a mess."

"I left my car here." She pointed to her now-clean car parked at the side of the house. "And I have someone coming out tomorrow to start the cleanup and landscaping—your friend, Tony."

"He told me." Jason raised a hand to Jim, who was locking up the garage. "Thanks, man. I'll be back later when I have the cash."

Jingling the keys in his palm, Jim joined her at the porch as Jason turned his truck around.

"You gave him a deal, didn't you?"

"He's a nice kid, really appreciative."

"Is your brother going to mind that you're selling one of the bikes for a steal?"

"Dax won't care as long as I leave him a few. He doesn't care about material things."

"Then why the crime?"

"Beats me. Excitement? A big snub to authority?"

She traced a crack in the wood handrail with her fingertip. "I wonder if it was the same for that gang of Quileute who was involved in drugs."

"Could be, not that I'm discounting money as a motivator for most criminals. It just never motivated Dax."

"So, the Quileute gang manufactured or procured drugs and sold them to the Lords of Chaos who turned around and sold them on the streets."

"Or distributed them elsewhere."

"And somehow the drugs and money are tied

to the kidnapping of three young children. How?" She picked at a piece of chipped paint.

"Trafficking maybe."

She clenched her teeth against the chill racing up her spine. "That's horrible."

"Sometimes the world is a horrible place." He covered her fidgeting hand with his own and his warmth seeped into her flesh. "Are you okay to go home by yourself?"

She flung out her other arm. "It's daytime. I'll be fine."

"I never did get the chance to install your new locks."

"Not that those locks would've protected me against the fire last night, and since the firefighters just left my place unsecured, the locks wouldn't have prevented the break-in, either."

"True, but that's no reason to ignore basic security measures. That was an extraordinary event last night."

"Funny thing about those extraordinary events."

"What?"

"They seem to be happening to me on an ordinary basis."

"Ever since the Timberline Trio case was unearthed."

"Pretty much." She disentangled her hand from his and pulled herself up by grasping the porch's handrail. "My cousin Annie is coming by to help me clean up this afternoon, so I won't be alone. I'm going to have a look for those childhood mementos."

"Looking for a pink ribbon?" He stood on the step above her, towering over her even more than usual.

"Yep."

"Be careful, Scarlett." He smoothed a hand down her arm. "Don't tell anyone about it."

"I'm not going to run around town blabbing it. I'm convinced there's not one person in Timberline who can keep a secret."

"Not even the sheriff's department."

She leaned back to look into his face. "Why do you say that?"

"How else did that story of the pink ribbon get out? If the kidnapper took something from one of the children, you'd think the police and the FBI would want to keep that quiet."

"It's the Quileute. We hear things. I'm pretty sure that info wasn't available to the other citizens of Timberline."

He bent forward and touched his forehead to hers. "Just be careful. We don't know who's watching and listening."

Her fingers dabbled against his jaw, and she felt his warm breath caress her cheek.

Then he wedged a finger beneath her chin and, tilting her head back, brushed his lips against hers.

The roar of a motorcycle engine broke them

apart, and Scarlett glanced over her shoulder at Dax, his long hair blowing behind him.

"What are you going to tell your brother about the tires?"

"I can't hide that the tires were slashed, but he doesn't have to know anything about what we discussed with your grandmother."

Dax parked his bike next to Jim's and circled the damaged motorcycle. Then he pulled off his helmet and shoved his sunglasses to the top of his head as he trudged to the porch.

"What the hell happened?"

"Someone took a knife or a box cutter to my tires at the reservation."

Whistling through his teeth, Dax shook his head. "Old resentments die hard, don't they?"

"Could've been teenagers." Jim shrugged his broad shoulders. "Reminded me of something you'd do."

"Guess so. How'd you get back here?"

Scarlett waved her hand in the direction of the road. "My cousin gave us a ride in his truck."

Jim descended the porch steps and buried his hands in his pockets. "I'm selling him one of Slick's bikes."

"That's cool, man."

"I'll give you half the proceeds."

"As long as you didn't sell him the two I was eyeing, I'm good." Dax rubbed his bloodshot eyes, the deep lines on his face making him look more like Jim's father than his older brother. "I'm gonna head inside and get some shut-eye. I'm beat."

Jim raised one eyebrow. "What've you been doing today?"

"Ridin'."

"Not using again?"

Dax chuckled. "I'm just old, brother. See you around, Scarlett."

"Thanks for washing my car."

He nodded and then tromped past them, his boots heavy on the steps. He closed the front door behind him with a slam.

Biting the side of his thumb, Jim stared at the door. "Something's not right with him."

"That applies to a lot of people around here." Scarlett dug her keys from her purse. "I'm going back to my place."

"When I get my tires changed, I'll come over and install those locks for you."

"I'll be there. Sorry about your bike, sorry it happened on the rez."

"Not your fault. I'm just wondering if we'd taken your car if the same thing would've happened."

"Something tells me it would have."

She slid into her car with her lips still tingling from Jim's soft kiss. She'd wondered what would've happened to her car if they'd taken it to the reservation, but even more, she was wondering what would've happened if Dax hadn't interrupted that kiss.

HER COUSIN ANNIE aimed the hose at the last window in the front, spraying water against the glass streaked with flame retardant. "They make a bigger mess putting out the fire than the fire itself."

"Not quite." When the water stopped, Scarlett scrubbed the window with a cloth and then sluiced the water off with a squeegee. "I really appreciate your help, Annie."

"I'm just glad you weren't hurt. Who would do something so stupid? This is just not your year."

"It's gotta get better, right?" She traced her bottom lip with her finger. Running into Jim this trip had just about made everything a little better.

Annie turned off the water and wound up the hose. "I think getting rid of all those trees in front of your place is a blessing in disguise. I never liked parking beyond the copse of trees and then walking through them on that path—creepy."

"But very private."

"Too private if you ask me. When's Tony coming out to clear the land?"

"Tomorrow. I'm hiring him to do some landscaping, too."

"Do you need me to do anything else? I'm meeting some friends in Port Angeles tonight and need to get going."

"No. I can do the rest. Thanks again."

She helped Annie pack up some of her cleaning supplies and load them into the van she used for her cleaning business. When she pulled onto the road, Scarlett turned toward the house. She'd skipped lunch, so she popped open a carton of yogurt and carried it to the hall closet, which she used for storage.

The cabin didn't have a garage, just a shed out back, but Scarlett didn't store much beyond paint supplies there. Any photos or newspaper clippings or cards she'd boxed and stashed on the top shelves of this closet.

She dragged a chair in front of the closet and pulled two boxes from the top shelf. Would she have kept something as inconsequential as a ribbon?

Once Granny brought it up, Scarlett remembered filching it from Granny's knitting basket. It had been important enough for her to steal back because of the way it had made her feel.

It was sort of like when she and her girlfriends would go out to the woods and spin around and around just to feel dizzy. Stroking the ribbon had given her the same sensation.

When Granny had sat her down and explained to her about the gift of the shamans, it had never occurred to Scarlett that the pink ribbon was momentous in that way.

Tucking one box under each arm, she returned to the living room and sat cross-legged on the floor in front of the fireplace. She pulled the first box toward her and rummaged through its contents.

She smiled at the photos and the cards she'd saved from friends and even tried jamming the promise ring she'd gotten from Tommy Whitecotton onto her pinky finger. But no pink ribbon was nestled among the memories.

She popped the lid from box number two and fished around inside. These photos and keepsakes were from her high school years. She thumbed through a stack of senior pictures, collected from her friends, and stopped at one of a serious, dark-haired boy.

She traced her finger over Jim's young face. She must've gotten up the courage to ask him for a picture. She flipped the photo over, but he hadn't signed it. Maybe she'd stolen it from him.

Giggling like a high school girl, she plucked the photo from the bunch and dropped it on the coffee table. He'd been such a hottie back then and had only gotten better with age.

She shuffled through the rest of the photos and keepsakes but didn't find a pink ribbon, or any ribbon. She replaced the lid on the second box and stacked one box on top of the other on the kitchen counter.

As she scraped up the last bit of yogurt with her spoon, a horn began to blare outside. She dropped the carton in the sink and flew to the front window. Sweeping the curtain aside, she peered through the glass at her own car sitting just beyond the burned logs and scorched trees.

Must be her horn, but it didn't sound like her car alarm. She grabbed her keys from her purse and, aiming the key fob in front of her, she jabbed the button to unlock the car door as she stepped outside and walked toward her wailing car.

She opened the door and blinked at the block of wood propped up on the seat and wedged against her horn.

"What the hell is this?" She hunched forward to knock the wood loose.

She sensed a whisper of movement, but before she could turn around someone shoved her face-first onto the passenger seat.

She screamed and struggled to turn her head.

A hand gripped the back of her neck, the thumb pressing close to her windpipe.

She tried to kick out behind her, but a body fell heavily on her back and the point of a knife pricked her throat just beneath her jawline.

She froze, her next scream turning into a whimper.

Hot breath and a hoarse whisper in her ear. "You've been warned. Leave it alone."

Chapter Twelve

Jim rolled up to Scarlett's cabin on a set of tires borrowed from another bike, enjoying the view. She'd be so much safer once the landscaper cleared the burned mess and passersby could see her cabin from the road.

His eyebrows collided over his nose as he took in Scarlett's car with the car door open wide. Then his heart started pumping double time when he saw her pointy-toed boots hanging out the door.

He parked behind her car and jumped off the bike. "Scarlett?"

As he reached the car door, she rolled over on her back and choked.

He took one look at her tear-streaked face, pale with fear, and grabbed her hands, yanking her out of the car and into his arms. Her body trembled against his.

"What in God's name happened? Are you hurt?"

Sniffling, she hauled in a couple of shaky breaths. "Someone just threatened me, held a knife to my throat."

His pulse jumped and he scooped her into a tighter hug. "How long ago? Why were you just lying in the car? Did he hurt you?"

"He didn't hurt me, but he told me to stay where I was. That was about five minutes ago. I'm sure he's long gone, but I was too afraid to move."

"Did you get a look at him?" Resting his chin on the top of Scarlett's head, he scanned the woods at the edge of her property. "What direction did he go?"

"I didn't hear a vehicle, so he must've come and gone on foot, which probably means through the forest. He wouldn't want to chance being seen from the road."

"You didn't get a look at him?"

"He approached me from behind and smashed my face into the car seat."

"How'd he do all that without revealing himself?"

"It…it was a trap." She kicked at a piece of wood on the ground. "He rigged this up to honk my horn. When I came out to investigate, he came up behind me. The horn was blaring and my ears were ringing, so I didn't hear him approach."

He combed his fingers through her long hair. "What did he want? Did he say anything?"

"He told me I'd been warned and to leave it alone. He obviously meant the Timberline Trio case."

He took her by the shoulders. "Do you want me to try to go after him?"

"No." She grabbed his jacket. "He had a head start, and he might…"

"I'm not afraid of him, Scarlett. He's a coward."

"You're not going to find him, Jim. Don't leave me here."

Cupping her face with one hand, he drew his thumb across her cheek. "I'm not going anywhere, but we need to call the sheriff's department."

"The man was wearing gloves. The cops aren't going to find anything."

"Let them worry about that. If he took off through the woods, he might've left evidence behind. Besides, didn't I tell you it's important to document all of these incidents?"

"The sheriff's department is going to deem me a public nuisance."

"Let 'em. They don't seem to be doing their jobs—murder, arson, vandalism. Where does it stop?"

"It stops when people give up on investigating the Timberline Trio."

He lifted the piece of wood on the ground with the toe of his boot and let it fall. "How does this person or people know you're looking into the case? I'm thinking it has to do with your association with me."

"My association with you? How do they know we're not just old friends, or…?"

"Something more?" His blood stirred at the thought of something more with Scarlett.

"Probably because we found a dead body together and visited your grandmother together."

"Maybe—" she twirled a strand of hair around her finger "—we should make people believe we're not just together to investigate the Timberline Trio."

He snapped his fingers. "Dinner tonight? In public?"

"That might do it. Of course," she said, and looked up at him through her dark lashes, "we have to make it look like more than just a business meeting."

He swallowed. "I can do that, but first let's get the cops out here."

Deputy Stevens came out to investigate and he and another deputy canvassed the woods but came up empty-handed.

They seemed to dismiss the connection to the Timberline Trio case and asked Scarlett a lot of questions about her known enemies—the hunters in the area, as she'd been known to sabotage their traps and protest expanded hunting areas.

When they left, she rolled her eyes at Jim.

"Law enforcement in this town seems to think I deserve these attacks because of my stance against hunting. I don't like hunters, but even I'll admit they're not violent types—against humans, anyway. We've exchanged words and heated arguments, but not one of them has ever attacked me."

"Could be a first."

"I've been too busy to protest much lately. Why would they turn violent on me now? No, this all started happening when I stepped in to help that reporter, Beth St. Regis, who was planning to do a segment on the Timberline Trio for her *Cold Case Chronicles* show."

"I thought you told me that was a cover for her own investigation into her past."

"It was, but nobody else knew that, except the FBI agent who was out here—Duke Harper."

Folding his arms, Jim wedged his hip against the post on the porch. "Do you think he'd talk to me about his findings when he was out here? Did you make that kind of connection with him?"

"I got friendly with him and Beth. They knew each other from before and are still together, as far as I know."

"Would you mind calling him for me or giving me his number?"

"Sure. I'll do that." She rubbed her throat, where an angry red mark remained as the only evidence of the attack she'd suffered. "Do you want to install those locks now?"

"Yeah, but I think you should upgrade to security cameras. If you'd had one, right now we'd be looking at the tape of the guy who assaulted you."

While he worked on the new locks, Scarlett retreated to her studio. When he poked his head into the room, she looked up from a laptop.

"Working?"

"Working, not creating. I'm doing an inventory of some pieces for my upcoming show."

"When's the show?" He weaved his way through the explosion of colors and textures in the room to reach the sliding door in the back.

"It's in a few weeks, in West Hollywood."

He pretended to concentrate on the sliding door. She had art shows all over the world. He'd looked her up on the internet. Critics raved about her modern art and high-end buyers snapped it up.

"What do you do with your cabin when you're away?"

"My cousins check in on it, and sometimes Jason stays here." She tapped her keyboard and closed the laptop. "Are you going home before we have dinner?"

"Yeah." He plucked his black T-shirt away from his chest. "I was wearing these clothes when I changed the tires on the bike. I won't be long. You hungry?"

Her eyes flicked over his body like a hot lash that he felt to his core. "Starving."

He finished his work in record speed as Scarlett wandered around the studio, assessing her work for the show. When he packed up his tools, he was more than ready to call it a day and spend some time with Scarlett—time where they wouldn't have to be looking over their shoulders every two minutes. Precious time before she left Timberline.

Hovering by the front door, he asked, "Do you want another spin on the bike, or do you want to drive?"

"I've had enough excitement for the day. I'll pick you up around seven."

He hesitated and then marched back to her. "Don't open the door for anyone, and don't go outside—not for a horn, not for an animal in distress."

"Thanks, you just made me scared to be in my own house." She bit her lip and glanced out the window.

"A little fear isn't a bad thing right now. Someone set fire to your property and someone physically threatened you." He folded his arms so he wouldn't be tempted to pull her against his chest again. There was no telling where that would end. "In fact, maybe you should think about heading down to California early for your show. Stop off in San Francisco on the way."

"Are you trying to get rid of me?"

"I'm trying to protect you, Scarlett. Let the sheriff's department handle Rusty's murder. Let me handle my own memories. I may not ever find out what happened that night, and maybe I'm not supposed to."

"I don't believe you'd be okay with that. It's the reason you returned to Timberline—you need to face all your demons."

He shook his head. "That could take years."

"Oh, wait." She held up her index finger. "I texted Dr. Shipman's number to you earlier. Did you get it?"

"I'm not sure. Do you want to give it to me again at dinner tonight?"

She rolled her eyes. "Lucky for you, I also wrote it down and stuck it to my fridge." She spun around and went into the kitchen, plucking a sticky note from the refrigerator.

With the yellow note stuck to her fingertip, she waved it at him as she returned. "Here you go."

"Thanks." He peeled the note from her finger and shoved it into his pocket. "See you at seven."

When Jim got back to his place, Dax was stretched out on the couch watching a fishing show.

Jim glanced at him out of the corner of his eye

as he tossed his keys on the kitchen table. "You been like that all afternoon?"

"I'm tired."

"Did you happen to run into Chewy when you were out today?"

"Matter of fact, I did drop in on him."

"So was it the stars aligning that brought the two of you back to Timberline at the same time? Rusty, too?"

"His woman's mother lives in Port Angeles. She's there visiting. Not much of a stretch for Chewy to come this way to check out his old stomping grounds. And I told you I don't know nothing about Rusty."

"Did you and Chewy talk about Rusty?"

"Uh-huh." Dax sat up. "Look at that fish. I need to do some fishing while I'm here…maybe some hunting."

Jim stopped at the entrance to the hallway, hooking a thumb in his front pocket. "You were never much for hunting."

Dax looked up, his hand buried in a bag of microwave popcorn. "That was you and Slick, wasn't it? He taught you to use a rifle like a pro. You put that knowledge to good use and started hunting another kind of animal."

Jim flinched. "I saved more lives than I took."

"I know that, J.T." Dax crammed a fistful of popcorn into his mouth. "Does that Scarlett feel the same way? She's out here in Timberline trying to save a few turkeys from their final resting place on the Thanksgiving dinner table. And you were over there…"

Jim banged his fist on the wall and shut out the rest of Dax's words by closing the bedroom door. As if he needed any more proof that Scarlett wouldn't want to start something with him.

Even if she *had* saved his high school senior picture.

SCARLETT VENTURED ONTO the porch, looking from left to right. She'd been spooked enough without Jim driving it home for her that someone had her in his crosshairs—just like prey.

She crept to her car and then slammed the door and locked it, releasing a long breath. She hated that someone had made her fear her own shadow, on her own property.

Pulling the car in front of Jim's cabin, she beeped the horn once. A rectangle of light appeared with the silhouette of Jim's body framed in the center.

As he descended the steps, she held her breath but didn't know why. His gait was more unsteady on steps, but he seemed to be able to navigate them with ease. He certainly didn't need her worrying about him.

She popped the locks as he approached, grabbed her purse from the passenger seat and shoved it on the floor of the backseat. As he slid in next to her, she breathed in the scent of soap and leather. The smell would always remind her of Jim forever after.

She blinked and forced a smile to her lips. "Sutter's? It's the place to see and be seen in town."

"That's the purpose behind this date."

"Date? Does that mean you're picking up the tab?" She tried to keep her tone light. Was showing others they were more than just investigative partners really the only purpose behind their dinner?

"I will absolutely pick up the tab. How'd it look otherwise?" He snapped on his seat belt.

"Like you're a cheapskate, so I'm glad we settled that."

"How much can rabbit food possibly cost? I'm guessing you're a cheap date."

She snorted. "You've obviously never shopped at health food stores."

She turned onto the main road to town and they drove in silence as Jim poked the radio buttons, never staying on a song for more than a few seconds. When they reached town, she parked in the public lot across from the restaurant.

Jim jumped from the car before she cut the engine and came around to the driver's side and opened the door. "Just getting into character."

She slid from the car and hooked her hand around his arm. "Me, too."

He opened the door of the restaurant for her, and several heads turned their way. That was the thing about small towns—everybody got up in your business. Maybe word would get around that they were dating and not together because they were poking their noses into kidnappings.

The hostess tapped her pencil on her notebook. "There's about a ten-minute wait right now unless you want to sit at the bar."

"We'll wait." Jim steered Scarlett toward the wall across from the hostess stand and gestured to the paintings decorating it. "Do you ever display your work here? Too lowbrow?"

"Not at all. I'll hang my landscapes of the area here occasionally. People like local art."

"But you wouldn't place your modern art here?"

"And scare everyone away? Nope."

They studied the artwork together until the hostess called them over.

"Your table is ready. Do you mind? It's kind of the center of the dining room. If you wait another ten minutes or so, I can probably seat you someplace more private."

"That's okay." Scarlett charged ahead to the only empty table in the place.

Jim pulled out a chair for her, and they both thanked the hostess.

Leaning forward, Jim asked, "Is Jason's girlfriend working tonight?"

"I have no idea." She looked around the room. "Doesn't look like it."

"Even though we're supposed to look like we're not talking about the Timberline Trio case," he said as he took her hand across the table, "doesn't mean we can't talk about it."

"Did your brother open up to you any more today?"

"No, but he did say he met with Chewy."

Her fingers toyed with his. "Your brother, Chewy and Rusty were all in town at around the same time and one of them ends up dead. Then Granny tells us that a couple of members of the old Q-gang show up out of the blue, including my uncle."

"I think they're all here for the same reason, and it has something to do with their association years ago at the time of the kidnappings."

"I think you're right, but nobody's talking."

The waiter approached their table and took their drink orders.

"You don't mind if I have a beer, do you?"

"No, but if you have more than one, I'll take the wheel on the way home."

"That's a deal. I'll probably need about five after the day I had." She held up her hands. "Just kidding."

"Go ahead and have five, Scarlett, if you want. I'm not a leading member of the temperance movement or anything."

"When did you give up drinking?"

"When I was in the army."

"Helluva time to swear off booze."

"You're telling me."

"Did you call Dr. Shipman this afternoon?"

"By the time I thought about it, she'd left for the day. I'll try again tomorrow."

The waiter returned with her beer and Jim's soda. "Are you ready to order?"

When they'd placed their orders and the waiter left, Jim asked, "You don't mind that I ordered pork chops, do you?"

"I'm not the leader of the vegetarian movement, either." She clinked her glass against his and took a sip of her beer.

Jim hunched forward and touched his finger to her upper lip. "Foam."

"Smooth move, Kennedy."

"That wasn't for show. You really did have some foam on your mouth."

She licked her lips. "What if you just gave it up? What if you just let that particular sleeping dog lie? Something unexplainable happened to you as a child. Can you let it go?"

"Not sure." He stirred his ice with his straw. "It haunted me when I was…imprisoned. Funny, all the things they did to me in captivity and my constant nightmare was the attempted kidnapping."

"Maybe because it happened to you as a child,

it holds a special terror. I'm not sure we ever get over our childhood fears."

"And what was yours? All I ever saw was a confident, pretty girl who knew what she wanted in life and went out to get it."

"I put up a good front." She took a long pull from her beer, savoring the warmth in her belly. "You know I lost my parents and my baby brother in a car accident. I was supposed to be in that car."

"I didn't know you had a brother. I'm sorry."

"He wasn't even a year old. I should've stopped all of them that day."

"How old were you?"

"Six, and before you start in with the 'you were too young' business, I believe that was my first experience with my special gift, only it wasn't so special."

"What do you mean?"

"I was supposed to be on that trip, but I faked a stomachache so I wouldn't have to go. I had a feeling, even back then."

He brushed his knuckles along her forearm. "And Evelyn was telling me to deal with my guilt. I hope she told you the same."

"I've worked through it. How do you think I know Dr. Shipman?"

"This is supposed to be a date. We're way too serious over here. People are going to have their suspicions confirmed that we're working on something together." He hunched forward on the table and kissed her mouth. "Do you think that'll convince them otherwise?"

"It's a start."

She wouldn't have minded practicing a little more convincing, but the waiter showed up with their food.

During their meal, they caught up on what they'd been doing since high school, and Jim's eyes lit up when he talked about his work with vets.

"You had a great idea before." She placed her fork on the edge of her plate. "Art."

"Sculpture?"

"Any kind of art—painting, sculpture, ceramics. Is there anything like that in any of the centers where you worked?"

"Not that I noticed, but I think that could work."

"I could probably get a fair number of my artist friends to volunteer some of their time."

"That would be incredible if you could provide the volunteers."

Smiling, Scarlett picked up her fork. Jim's approval gave her a warm feeling inside. She cut off a corner of her spinach lasagna. His approval was coming to mean a lot to her—maybe too much. He had demons to slay and she had an art show in West Hollywood.

"Hey there, Scarlett."

She dropped her fork as she met the dark gaze of her uncle, a little frisson of fear glancing the back of her neck. He'd appeared out of nowhere, just like he always did, stealthy as a cat.

"Uncle Danny. Are you back in town?"

He spread his arms, his eyes flickering toward Jim. "I'm here, aren't I?"

"I—I just didn't hear anything about your return." She gritted her teeth at the way her voice wavered, but she had no intention of admitting she and Granny had talked about him. Her uncle could reduce her to a stammering child with one look from his cold eyes—even when she wasn't lying to him.

"You shouldn't depend on the reservation grapevine." He formed his fingers into a gun and aimed it at her. "It's usually wrong."

"I'm sorry." She tipped her head toward Jim. "This is Jim Kennedy. He's a local. I went to high school with him. Jim, this is Danny Easton, my uncle."

"I remember the Kennedy family—Slick and your brother. You a bigot, too?"

Scarlett drew in a quick breath, her eyes darting to Jim's face.

Jim pushed his plate away and crossed his arms over his chest. "I guess they weren't too bigoted for you and your boys to do some business with them."

Scarlett held her breath as Danny's lips formed a thin line and his black eyes glittered.

"Sounds like you've been listening to gossip from the rez, too." He drummed his long fingers on the table. "I'd join you, Scar, but I'm meeting someone at the bar."

"Are you going to drop in on Granny while you're here?"

"Why? She never liked me. Never thought our family was good enough for your mother."

Scarlett dropped her gaze to her plate and twirled the tines of her fork around a string of melted cheese. "She never had a problem with Dad."

Danny released a soft snort, and the heels of his boots clicked away from the table.

"No family love there, huh?"

"Uncle Danny is no friend to the Quileute. He's always been bad news. When my mom and dad started dating, Granny was concerned about her marrying into the Easton family, but like I said, she judges everyone individually. When she met my dad, she could tell he was one of the good guys—Danny, not so much."

"I don't remember Danny, and I sure don't remember that he had some gang of his own."

"That surprised me, too, but I do know that he was persona non grata around the reservation. After the accident that killed my parents, I never saw him."

"So, another piece of the puzzle moves into position. We have Rusty, Chewy and my brother all converging on Timberline and now Danny Easton shows up. It's like a dark cloud hovering over the town." He shook the ice in his glass. "I suppose you'd have known if it was your own uncle holding a knife to your neck, wouldn't you?"

"I would, but you know what's unsettling?"

"Let's see." He held up his hand and ticked off his fingers. "Finding a dead body, arson, a defaced painting and a knife attack?"

"Besides all that." She picked up her butter knife and ran her thumb along the dull, serrated edge. "The man who attacked me was wearing gloves."

"*That* was the most unnerving aspect of the whole event?"

"Gloves, so he avoided skin-to-skin contact with me."

"It wouldn't be unusual for someone planning an attack like that to include gloves in his kit. And if he's the same one who killed Rusty and broke into your place, we already know he doesn't leave fingerprints."

"I know that, but there's another reason why he'd wear gloves in an attack on me—there's always the chance that I'll flash on him. You know, feel his touch and be able to determine something about him."

"So you think it's someone who knows you or knows about your special gifts."

"Uncle Danny knows all about that—and how those gifts work."

Jim jerked his thumb over his shoulder. "Can you see who he's meeting at the bar?"

"He's behind the wall that separates that half of the bar from the dining room. I can't see him."

"Trip to the ladies' room? Men's room is on the other side."

"Good idea." Scarlett swept her napkin from her lap and dropped it beside her plate. She didn't even have to be obvious about spying on Danny, since she could walk to the ladies' room through the dining room without passing through the bar. She turned left into the passageway to the restroom, without looking into the bar.

While she washed her hands, she peered into the mirror to make sure she didn't have any spinach in her teeth. She was still treating this as a date, even though it had veered off its intended course with the appearance of Uncle Danny.

She tossed a paper towel into the trash and then hit the swinging door with her hip to open it. She meant to glance quickly to her right just to check out Danny and his companions, but what she saw halted her in her tracks and made her blood boil.

She swerved into the bar and poked her cousin Jason in the back. "What are you doing with him?"

Danny's lips curled into a half smile and Jason jumped. "Scarlett. What are you doing here?"

"I'm having dinner with Jim. More to the point, what are *you* doing here and what are you doing with Danny?"

"I—I just came in to pick up a check for Chloe, who's not feeling well, and I ran into your uncle."

"Really? Because he just got through telling me he was meeting someone here."

Danny patted her shoulder. "I am, Scarlett, and it's not Jason. Relax. I'm not corrupting your cousin. Besides, shouldn't you be more worried about J.T. and Dax Kennedy corrupting him? At least I'm not an ex-con."

"Doesn't mean you shouldn't be." She shook her finger in Jason's face. "Whatever he's offering, it's sure to have a high price down the road. It's not worth it. Just keep doing what you're doing, Jason."

She spun around as Danny called after her. "Always nice to see you, Scar."

She flounced back to the table and dropped into her chair.

"What happened? Who's Danny meeting?"

"My cousin Jason."

"Is Danny his uncle, too?"

"No, Jason and Annie are my mom's brother's kids—Fosters, not Eastons."

"You don't want Jason associating with Danny?"

"Danny doesn't show interest in family unless he thinks he can get something out of it. I'm just worried he's filling Jason's head with all kinds of get-rich-quick schemes—illegal get-rich-quick schemes."

Jim shifted forward, his knees bumping hers beneath the table. "Jason seems like he's got his head on straight."

"Yeah, but construction work has been slowing down for him, and Chloe's still trying to finish school, but she had to drop out last semester. Money's tight for them, and I know how persuasive Uncle Danny can be."

"Do you want me to talk to Jason?" Jim's lips twisted. "I have some experience in resisting the dark forces around me."

"Would you?" She grabbed his hand. "That would be awesome."

"He's coming by to look at his bike tomorrow. I'll give him an earful then." He raised her hand to his lips and kissed her knuckles. "This hasn't been much of a romantic date, has it?"

"Honestly?" She brushed her fingertips across his dark stubble. "This has been one of the best dates I've had in a long time."

"Those artist types must be a dull bunch, but just to amp up the romance—I paid the check while you were sleuthing in the bar."

"Positively makes my heart flutter."

"Imagine what I could do if I really tried."

As she met his smoldering gaze, her heart really did flutter.

She grabbed her purse. "I'm ready to get out of here."

"Me, too."

As Scarlett rose from her chair and squeezed past a table on her way to the exit, Darcy Kiesling, an old friend from high school, stopped her. "I heard someone attacked you today. Are you all right?"

"I'm okay. It was a threat, not exactly an attack."

"I don't care what you call it. Someone held a knife to your throat." Darcy pressed a hand to her own throat. "Did the guy really warn you about looking into the Timberline Trio case?"

"Maybe." Scarlett shrugged. "I don't know why he's warning me. I'm not looking into anything."

"Hmm, I wish that whole thing would go away." Darcy's gaze tracked to Jim and she gave him a head-to-toe.

"Darcy, do you remember Jim Kennedy?"

"I do, and do you remember Renée Meyers?"

After they said hello to Renée, Darcy introduced them to the other two women at the table. Only Renée was a local. The other two were recent transplants, but from the way all of them were eyeing Jim, it was clear the man was just as sexy as the boy had been—more so.

Darcy flipped her hair over her shoulder. "What happened to your leg, Jim?"

"It's a long story, Darcy, and I don't want to ruin your dinner. Enjoy your evening."

He limped away from the table and Scarlett smiled sweetly. "Good night."

She caught Jim by the arm as they stepped onto the sidewalk. "I think you just *did* ruin their dinner."

"Was I too harsh?"

"Just a little." She held her thumb and forefinger about a half an inch apart. "Does it bother you when people ask about your leg?"

"I can understand the curiosity, especially from people who knew me before. It's just not a subject for polite discussion. Do you really think Darcy and her tipsy friends want to hear what happened to me in that hole?"

Scarlett stopped walking and tugged on Jim's back pocket to slow him down. "They probably don't want to hear, but I'm all ears if you ever want to unburden yourself."

Stepping toward her, he put his hands on either side of her waist. "I'd never do that to you, Scarlett. It's bad enough that you experience snatches of it whenever I touch you."

He dropped his hands as if he was in danger of having his mind read right then and there.

"It's not whenever you touch me." She laced her fingers through his and put his hand back on her hip. "I can assure you, when you touch me I'm not thinking about prisoner of war camps and torture."

"What are you thinking of?" He drew her into the circle of his arm, so close that strands of her hair caught on the stubble of his beard.

She whispered, "Sometimes I can't think at all."

When he kissed her, she melted against him, her knees weakening and her bones turning to jelly. She curled her hands around the leather of his jacket to keep from sliding to the ground while returning his kiss.

He murmured against her mouth, "Let's go back to your place."

She nodded once, and they practically ran to her car.

He stopped her at the driver's side and held out his hand. "I'll drive."

"It was just one beer."

He snapped his fingers and she dropped the keys into his palm. He followed her to the other side of the car and opened the door for her.

She'd never been with such a take-charge guy

before. When Jim had landed on her porch a few days ago, she'd actually had the thought that he'd be just another man for her to prop up and nurture.

He couldn't have proved her more wrong.

Yeah, he still had those demons, but he seemed completely capable of battling them without any help from her.

That didn't mean she couldn't offer.

As he turned off the main road, he said, "I'm going to swing by my place first, if that's okay. I want to make sure Dax locked up the garage when he finished working on his bike."

"Okay, but you don't need to bring your toothbrush. I have extras."

"Is that a dig at me because I didn't have any extras when you stayed here?"

"Actually, I was happy to see that you weren't prepared for overnight…guests."

He pulled into his drive and leaned over and pinched her chin. "I wish I had been more prepared for you—in every way."

"If you'd been prepared, that would've ruined all the excitement."

"You like excitement? I think we've had more than enough of that around here."

"Isn't that what you signed up for when you decided to come back and find out what happened to you twenty-five years ago?"

"I didn't realize there would be people today hell-bent on keeping that truth from me."

"Makes you wonder what they're hiding."

He tapped on the windshield. "Good thing we swung by here. I can see already that Dax left that garage door wide open…unless he's still working out there."

"Let's find out." She hopped out of the car, which rocked as Jim slammed his door.

"Dax?" Jim strode toward the garage, while she hung back.

Drops of rain started hitting the ground and pinging the top of her head. Head down, she jogged toward the covered porch. As she reached the top step, the wind gusted and rattled the screen door.

She jerked her head to the side, noticing the open front door. Taking one step down on the porch, she yelled, "Jim! I think he's inside."

She studied the entrance to the garage, but Jim didn't answer or appear.

She returned to the front door, made a half turn and grabbed the screen door handle, her hand closing around a sticky substance. She snatched her hand back and spread her fingers in front of her face.

The sight of the blood smeared across her palm made her gag. She ignored the faint voice in her head urging her to turn and run.

As if on autopilot, she reached for the screen

door again with the same hand. She yanked it open and almost tripped over the booted feet of Jim's brother—lying on the floor in a pool of blood.

Chapter Thirteen

For the second time that week, a bloodcurdling scream from Scarlett made the hair on the back of his neck stand at attention.

Jim dropped the shredded tire he'd been inspecting and spun around, keeping his bum leg stiff so he wouldn't trip over it.

He ran toward the house, where he could see Scarlett's back at the door. With his heart pounding out of his chest, he raced up the drive and took both steps in a single bound.

He grabbed Scarlett's shoulders and yanked her back against his chest.

His gut heaved when he saw Dax laid out on the floor, blood meandering in a slick trail leading from his body. He shoved his phone into Scarlett's hand.

"Call 911."

He crouched beside his brother and felt for his pulse, weak but ticking. "He's still alive."

He rolled Dax onto his back and ripped off his shirt, already slashed open with a knife.

"Get me a towel."

Still speaking into the phone, Scarlett stepped over Dax's inert form and returned seconds later with several towels.

She thrust one toward Jim. "An ambulance is on the way."

Jim folded the towel and pressed it against the wound that zigzagged from his brother's chest to his belly. If the knife had hit an artery, Dax didn't stand a chance.

Jim applied as much pressure as he safely could while whispering to his brother, "Hang on, man. You've come too far to let go."

"Can I do anything? He has some cuts on his hands. Should I put pressure on those?"

Sirens called from down the road and Jim said, "Go out and direct the ambulance into the driveway."

She sprang to her feet and stumbled outside.

A minute later, two EMTs bustled through the front door and nudged Jim away from Dax. "Good job. We'll take it from here."

Jim backed up, leaving the towel in place. He gazed at his hands, stained with Dax's blood.

"Any other wounds? Any allergies? Preexisting conditions?" The EMT in charge rattled off the series of questions in staccato.

"Some cuts on his hands. No allergies. No preexisting conditions, unless you count drug and alcohol addictions."

"Current?"

"Recovering—about a year sober."

More sirens followed and Jim staggered out the front door and down the steps, his bloody hands in front of him.

Scarlett left the deputy's side to rush to his. "Is he still…?"

"He's still alive but unconscious."

One of the EMTs blew past him on his way to the ambulance and Jim watched as he rolled a gurney out the back doors.

Just like for Rusty, but Jim prayed for a different outcome this time.

The deputy was mouthing words at him, but Jim couldn't make sense out of anything he was saying.

As the EMTs loaded Dax into the ambulance, Jim broke away from Scarlett.

"I'm coming with."

"We need to work on him in the back. Follow us to the emergency room."

Scarlett joined him and pressed a fresh towel into his hands. "You take my car. I'll finish talking to the deputy and we'll meet you at the hospital."

Wiping his hands on the towel, he nodded and returned to the car where he and Scarlett had just shared some moments of closeness.

He gulped as he threw the car into Reverse. She had to get out of here, away from Timberline. She had to demonstrate to the perpetrator of this mayhem that she had no interest in the Timberline Trio case. But for him?

This had just gotten personal, and he'd go to hell and back to find out who'd tried to murder Dax. He'd already been to hell and back once. What was one more trip?

He followed the revolving lights of the ambulance, mumbling the same prayers he'd recited each time his captors had dragged another prisoner from the cells, prayers that hadn't done a lot of good back then. He couldn't do anything else for Dax at this point, but the attack on his brother had just amped up his resolve to get to the bottom of this mystery.

The ambulance pulled up to the entrance of the emergency room, and Jim swung around it to find a parking space in the lot to the left of the hospital.

By the time he had parked and returned to the entrance, the EMTs had already unloaded Dax and wheeled him into the building.

He hunched over the reception desk. "That ambulance just brought my brother in—Dax Kennedy. Can you tell the doctor in charge I'm here and will be waiting for news?"

The nurse took down his info and went back to her computer.

Jim wandered around the waiting room, studying the vending machine, getting a cup of water and shuffling through a few golf and hunting magazines.

He tapped on the counter. "Any news yet?"

"No, sir." This time she didn't even look up from her computer.

Heaving out a breath, he slumped in a plastic chair next to a woman flipping through a fishing magazine, her face tight and her knuckles white.

The door of the emergency room burst open and Scarlett rushed through with Deputy Stevens on her heels. She flung herself into the chair next to him, bringing the damp, cold air in with her.

"Have you heard anything? Is Dax okay?"

"Nope, and I haven't talked to anyone yet, either."

She tipped her head toward the deputy talking to the nurse at the front desk. "Maybe he'll have better luck. He wants to talk to the doctor."

"Did Dax say anything to you, or was he already unconscious?"

"He was already unconscious."

"You didn't see or notice anything?"

"No. Was there anything in the garage?"

"Dax had left his tools and a motorcycle part on the floor, sort of like he'd been called away suddenly. I figured he'd gone in the house to get something to drink or answer the phone. Thought you'd find him inside."

"I did." Her jaw tightened.

"Scarlett, you need to—"

"Mr. Kennedy?"

Jim jerked his head around and answered the doctor who'd stepped into the waiting room. "Yeah, that's me."

He crossed the room with Scarlett beside him and the deputy tagging along behind them.

"I'm Dr. Verona." He pushed up his glasses and rubbed his eyes. "It's bad. Your brother lost a lot of blood."

"Is he going to make it?"

"Can't say right now. He's in a coma. We're going to transfer him to a bed in the intensive care unit in the hospital next door."

"Can you tell me his chances at this point?"

"Fifty-fifty, maybe less. I've seen worse survive, and I've seen better succumb."

"So, you're telling me it's pretty much a crapshoot at this point."

"I'm afraid so. No major organs involved, so that's a plus."

The doc went on to explain Dax's condition in greater detail, but all Jim heard was fifty-fifty. His brother had beaten those odds before, and Jim had faith that he could do it again.

Although he hadn't seen Dax in years, he wasn't ready to lose him now. "His girlfriend. He has a girlfriend who's in Seattle right now. I should call her. Do you have his personal effects?"

"The nurse can help you with that. I'll transition your brother to the ICU tomorrow morning and have his doctor there give you a call."

"I appreciate it, Dr. Verona. Can I look in on him here?"

"Of course. I'll have the nurse bring you back."

As the doctor turned, Deputy Stevens held up his hand. "Can I ask you a few questions, Dr. Verona? We're treating this as an attempted homicide."

The doctor pointed to the left. "We can go in that office, but I just have a few minutes."

When they disappeared into the office, Jim leaned against the counter and addressed the nurse. "Dr. Verona said I could go back and see my brother."

She held up her finger, and then picked up the phone. "Tell Tiana the brother wants to see five twenty-eight."

Jim lifted his eyebrows and Scarlett said, "His name is Dax."

"Sorry." The nurse spread her hands. "It's just a shortcut. He received excellent care. Dr. Verona's the best trauma doc around."

The door to the exam and operating rooms swung open and a nurse in pink scrubs poked her head out. "Are you Dax's brother? This way."

Jim grabbed Scarlett's hand. "She's my wife, and she's coming with me."

The nurse rolled her eyes. "No, she's not. She's

Scarlett Easton, and I know for a fact she's not married, but she can come, anyway."

"Tiana…" Scarlett snapped her fingers. "Your grandmother and mine were friends for years."

"That's right—Gokey. Tiana Gokey. I didn't grow up here because my parents left the reservation, but I moved back here when my grandmother was ill and I stayed."

"Thanks for letting me check in on Jim's brother. I—I'm the one who found him."

"It's a good thing you two acted quickly. If he lives, it's because you stanched that flow of blood." Tiana pulled aside a curtain and Jim's eye twitched at the sight of his brother with tubes running in and out of him, hooked up to machines.

"The doc said Dax had a fifty-fifty chance."

"If that's what Dr. Verona said, it's probably close. He's the best." She stuck a chart in a holder at the foot of the bed. "We'll be moving him out of the emergency wing to the main hospital in the morning. Take your time."

"Thanks, Tiana." Jim dragged a plastic chair next to his brother's bed, his gaze tracking along the tubes and monitors crisscrossing Dax's body. "He looks bad."

Scarlett stood beside him and squeezed his shoulder. "Shh. He may be able to hear us. Be positive."

Jim leaned close to his brother's pale face and

murmured a few words of encouragement, talked to him the way he might talk to one of the vets he worked with.

"God, I hope he pulls out of this."

"We just have to have some faith and think positive thoughts." Scarlett reached past him and twitched Dax's sheet into place, her hand skimming his arm.

She jerked back with a gasp.

"What's wrong?" Jim narrowed his eyes. "You felt something, didn't you?"

Scarlett stared at her fingers, which trembled in front of her face. "I flashed on something."

"Hopefully, the face of my brother's assailant."

"Not quite. Just…something." She wiggled her fingers. "I could try again."

"Not if it's going to upset you." He held his breath, torn between wanting any information Scarlett could glean and wanting to protect her from harm.

Scarlett nudged the sheet aside and curled her fingers around Dax's hand, over the tubes stuck in his flesh. Closing her eyes, she exhaled a long breath. Her chin dropped to her chest and her breath quickened. Her lashes fluttered.

The curtain across the doorway whipped back, and Scarlett yanked her hand back.

"I'm sorry." Tiana smiled brightly as she grasped the curtain. "We have to run a few tests on Dax before we send him over tomorrow morning."

Jim scooted his chair back, blocking Tiana's view of the bed. "Sure, sure. Thanks for letting me see him."

Out of the corner of his eye, he glanced at Scarlett, blinking and pushing her hair back from her damp forehead.

She patted Dax's hand and straightened the sheet. "Hang in there, Dax."

They walked silently out to the reception area where Deputy Stevens was waiting for them.

"Do you need anything else from us, Quentin?"

"Kennedy, can you come into the station tomorrow? I just want to ask you a few more questions about your brother. Another Lord was spotted around town—Charles Swanson—Chewy. You know him?"

"Yeah."

"He and your brother on good terms?"

"I have no idea, Stevens. Can we leave this for tomorrow like you said?"

"Yeah. You two going to be okay? It's like a mini crime wave between your properties out there."

"You're telling me. I'm assuming my cabin is an active crime scene right now?"

"That's right."

Scarlett tugged on the sleeve of his jacket. "You can stay at my place tonight."

That had been their original plan, and it sounded

even better now. If Stevens was surprised at Scarlett's easy invitation, his stoic face didn't show it.

"That's probably a good idea, since we still don't have a lead on the arsonist, and he might very well be the same person who threatened you the other night and then stabbed Dax today."

Jim scratched his chin. "Busy…busy and desperate."

"For what? I can't believe a twenty-five-year-old cold case is still causing this much havoc." Stevens clapped his hat on his head.

"If the perpetrators of the kidnapping are still here and have something to lose, they're going to want to shut up everyone involved."

"Are you saying your brother was involved? Scarlett? She was just a kid, and so were you."

"Yeah, well, kids sometimes know more than adults give them credit for."

"All right. I'll let you go. I notified Sheriff Musgrove, so check in with us tomorrow, Kennedy."

"Will do." Jim propelled Scarlett out the main entrance and toward her car. When they were both ensconced inside, he turned to her. "Did you see anything when you touched Dax?"

"Nothing. I was just getting started when Tiana interrupted me." She drummed her fingers against her chin. "Hadn't she just told you to take your time?"

"You know how hospitals are." He paused.

"What are you saying? Do you think Tiana stopped you on purpose?"

"She's Quileute. She knows what I am."

"So, she might be trying to protect someone."

"Like I told you before, there's something about this case that always had my people on edge."

"Doesn't seem to have your uncle Danny on edge."

"I'm going to have to pay a visit to Jason tomorrow to find out what Danny was up to tonight."

"Do you think he'll tell you?"

"I have my ways." Scarlett cracked her knuckles and winked. "Now, let's get going. You must be exhausted."

"I'm still doing better than Dax."

As JIM CRANKED on the engine and then pulled out of the hospital's driveway, Scarlett tipped her head back against the headrest. How had their evening gone from delicious to deadly?

And how could she get it back to delicious?

She sighed, and Jim bumped her shoulder with his. "Would you rather I stay at a hotel tonight and leave you in peace?"

"Peace? What's that?"

"I'd do it, except I don't think you should be alone in that cabin—not with everything that's going on right now."

"I don't want to be alone, Jim." She turned to him and traced a finger along the seam of his jeans running along his thigh. "I have an idea."

She'd lowered her voice to almost a whisper, and he dipped his head to the side to catch her words. "Tell me."

"There's a nice, shiny hotel in the new area of town near Evergreen. It has a hot tub, a bar—for me—king-size beds, and the best thing of all? No dead bodies outside and no fire circling the building."

He paused at the intersection, the *tick-tick* of the turn signal breaking the silence. "Would you feel safe at this hotel?"

"With you, yes."

He bumped the indicator down with his fist and made the left turn instead of the right. "Take me there."

She called out directions to the hotel until he pulled into the parking lot.

"Looks nice."

"It's a little pricey, but much better than the dumps near the center of town."

Jim used his credit card to check in and, after Scarlett made sure the hot tub was still open and the bar was still serving, they made their way to their room on the third floor.

Jim shrugged out of his jacket and hooked his thumb through his belt loop. "You keep mentioning this hot tub, but as far as I can tell neither one of us has a swim suit."

"Shh." She put her finger to her lips. "I think we can sneak down there and wear our underwear. There won't be anyone there at this time of night."

"I always knew you were a rebel." He sat on the edge of the bed and wasted no time pulling off his boots.

Scarlett grabbed two thick towels from the bathroom, slung one over her shoulder and tossed the other to Jim. "Just in case there aren't any at the pool."

Barefoot, in their jeans and T-shirts, they made their way to the lobby on the first floor and turned the corner for the gym and indoor pool, and for the first time in a long time, Scarlett really did feel like a rebel.

She cupped her hand above her eyes and pressed her nose to the glass, peering into the pool area. "Empty—just the way I like it."

Jim swiped his card key at the door and pushed it open when the green light blinked at them.

The moist air settled on Scarlett's skin, and she dipped a toe in the pool as she walked along its edge. "The water's warm."

"That water's warmer." Jim pointed to the hot tub, in the corner, steam rising from its surface.

Scarlett rested her hand on the tile and poked

her head inside the hot tub enclosure. "Nice and private, too."

"Let's keep the towels close by, just in case." He dropped his towel on the edge of the hot tub and glanced over his shoulder before peeling off his T-shirt.

The steam from the hot tub warmed her cheeks, or maybe it was just the sight of Jim's muscled torso—battered and scarred, but still beautiful.

"Let's get this party started." He twisted a dial on the wall and the jets churned the water in the tub.

Jim yanked off his jeans and slid onto the top step in one fluid motion, his boxers floating above his thighs.

"You're fast." She slipped her arms from the sleeves of her T-shirt and then tugged it over her head. Her bra, nothing fancy, actually covered more than a bikini top would. So why did she feel so bare beneath Jim's hungry gaze?

"Here goes nothin'." She pulled off her jeans and stepped into the hot tub, the thin material of her underwear clinging and molding to her body as she submerged herself in the water.

Her knees bobbed against his, and he reached for her hands. "Join me on this side. This way we can both keep an eye on the door."

Her body floated in the bubbling water as he pulled her to the other side. She settled on the step beside him, resting the back of her head against the edge of the hot tub.

The jets pummeled her lower back and she stretched her legs and wiggled her toes against the bubbles across the tub.

"This feels heavenly. I can almost forget everything that's happened the past few days."

"Everything?" He draped an arm across her shoulders, the tips of his fingers dabbling a pattern on her arm. "Even this…electricity between us?"

"If we give in to this—" she flicked some water at his chest "—thing between us, how's it going to end?"

"It's gonna end with me making mad, passionate love to you."

The hot water got hotter and she wriggled in closer to him on the step, her thigh brushing his. "Not that I have any objection at all to making love—especially the mad, passionate kind—but what happens when you get your answers? When you sell your dad's place? When you go to school somewhere?"

"When you take off for your next art show?"

She nodded and then wedged her chin on his shoulder, the steam rising from his skin making her blink—it couldn't be tears.

"I don't know. I can only give you the here and now. I don't even know what's going to happen in a day or two, but I do know that I want you."

He growled softly in her ear. "I know that I want to be inside you."

She gave a little shiver and slipped farther beneath the water, her fingers digging into his thigh for leverage.

"But I understand if you don't want to go there with me if I can't promise you anything more. Hell, maybe that's the answer you're looking for. Maybe you don't want to be saddled with a beat-up vet like me for the long haul, anyway."

With a quick glance at the door to the pool area, she swung around to face him, straddling his lap with her legs. She put a finger to his lips and then replaced it with a wet kiss.

"You couldn't be more wrong, and it makes me wonder how you can possibly make mad, passionate love to me when you don't seem to understand the first thing about me or what I want."

He cinched her waist with his hands. "So, you're looking for something long-term, or you don't care if this is a fling?"

"For a guy, you're analyzing this way too much." She scooted against him and felt his erection swell against her inner thigh. "Or maybe not."

Slipping his hands beneath the elastic waistband of her panties, he smoothed his palms across her bottom, his fingers kneading her flesh.

She dipped her head to his chest and ran the tip of her tongue along the jagged scar that marred his smooth skin, as she rocked her hips against him.

He groaned and dragged his fingers over her hip to pull aside the skimpy material of her underwear. Sighing, she fell forward and lodged her head in the hollow between his neck and shoulder.

Closing her eyes, she held her breath as the warm, bubbling water coursed over her sensitive flesh now laid bare. Then he took two fingers and drew them across her skin, leaving a trail of fire that she felt even under the hot water.

She took a quick peak over her right shoulder. "Do you think it's safe?"

"I'll keep my eyes on the door and my hands on your body. How's that?" He caressed her again and then slipped his fingers inside her.

She collapsed against him again, curling her arms around his neck. Jim really was a bad boy. This was exactly the sort of behavior all the girls' parents had been worried about—and rightly so.

As his fingers explored her, his thumb swept back and forth across her throbbing flesh, stoking the flame in her belly. She pressed her lips against his throat, where a pulse hammered wildly.

She dropped her hand between their bodies to where his fingers were toying with her, teasing her, driving her mad.

He captured her fingers. "Do you want to feel how hot you are?"

Before she could peel her tongue from the roof of her mouth to answer, he replaced his fingers with hers and she could feel her own burgeoning desire. With his hand driving her own, she stroked herself. Then he brought her hand to his lips and kissed her palm.

He continued to wind her up as she trailed her fingers along the length of his erection. He might be a broken-down vet as he liked to call himself, but he had a lot of full-functioning parts.

Her muscles tensed, she gripped his hips with her thighs and then the wave of passion cresting in her body broke and she fell apart. As she rocked against him, riding out her orgasm, the water lapped between their bodies.

Cupping her face with his hands, he kissed the tremulous sighs from her lips. When the last spasm of pleasure slipped away and melted in the water, she dragged her fingernails lightly across the tight flesh of his erection.

He wrapped his fingers around her wrist. "Let's finish this party on the bed, in the room, behind a locked door. Once I start with you, I don't think I'm going to be able to stop—interruption, or no interruption."

With the tip of her tongue, she caught a droplet of water meandering down his chest. "Is what we just did illegal?"

"If there had been anyone in the pool area, I'm sure it would've been, but if you don't tell, I won't." He ran his hands across the silky material of her underwear, smoothing it into place. Then he flicked up the straps of her bra.

"Don't bother." She stilled his hands with her own. "I'm not going to put my nice, dry clothes on over these sopping wet undergarments."

He lifted one eyebrow. "You plan to wear those sopping wet undergarments through the lobby, or pull off another Lady Godiva?"

"We'll take them off, dry off and put on our dry clothes." She brushed her thumb across his lower lip. "We'll wrap up our undies in the towels and nobody will notice a thing."

"You've done this before?" Lifting his backside from the step, he peeled off his boxers and balled them in his fist.

She coughed as her gaze swept over his nakedness beneath the water. "Have you?"

"You seem to be the expert."

"Just using my common sense." She tapped the side of her head.

"Might as well get it over with." Hunching forward, he reached for his towel, steam rising from his back and buttocks, water coursing over the intricate design of his tattoo and his hardened muscles.

Scarlett's lashes fluttered and butterflies claimed her belly. However things turned out with his man, she'd have no regrets about this night.

Jim toweled off his upper torso and then stepped from the hot tub to finish the job. He wrapped the towel around his waist and pulled on his jeans beneath the towel.

"You're right." He dropped the towel and shook out his T-shirt. "This feels a lot better than wearing wet boxers."

"Looks a lot better, too." She winked.

He held out her towel. "You going to float in there all night ogling me, or are you going to get dressed?"

"I could do just that, Jim Kennedy, but I'm going to do more than ogle when we get up to the room." She shimmied out of her underwear and stood up on the top step.

Jim stepped between her and the door to the pool area. "Just in case someone decides on a late-night swim."

"Oh, is that what people do in here?" She snorted and dried off her body.

Jim came up behind her and yanked her T-shirt over her head.

She copied him by wrapping the towel around her waist and putting on her jeans. She squeezed out her wet underclothes and rolled them up in the towel. "There. Now we won't have our wet stuff seeping into our dry stuff."

"It won't take us long to get back to the room, anyway."

"I'm going to make a stop at the bar for a glass of wine, if that's okay with you."

"As long as you get it to go." He flipped the ends of her damp hair over her shoulder. "Because I'm not waiting another minute for you, Scarlett Easton."

Leaning forward on her tiptoes, she pressed her damp bundle into his arms and kissed his lips. "Do you mind taking my clothes to the room? I'd hate to have them fall out of the towel in the middle of the bar."

"That could definitely be awkward."

When they stepped into the hallway, leaving the humid atmosphere of the indoor pool, Scarlett shivered. She'd felt safe and protected in the hot tub with Jim, and the cool air in the hallway was like a cold dose of reality. She hugged herself. Soon they'd be wrapped in each other's arms making love...and she'd feel safe again.

They paused at the elevator bank and Jim stabbed the button. "Do you have money?"

"I'm going to put it on the room—three eighty-two, right?"

"That's the one. Are you sure you don't want me to go with you or wait here? You know I can be in a bar and not go crazy?"

"I know that. You can lay out our clothes so they'll be dry by tomorrow morning, and maybe get a hot shower going." The elevator dinged as it settled at the lobby level. "I'll be right up."

She waved to him as the doors closed and then spun around toward the lobby. She crossed the room, making a beeline for the dark bar in the corner, which was emitting live folk music.

Who knew Timberline had an actual nightlife? Evergreen Software really had changed the town.

She walked to the entrance of the bar, her bare feet sinking into the carpet. A couple deep in conversation didn't even look up when she entered. The lone guy at the bar gave her a quick glance before turning his attention back to the silent TV screen, and a woman seated in front of the musician gave Scarlett a dirty look and put her finger to her lips—must be the folk singer's girlfriend. So much for Timberline nightlife.

Scarlett ordered a glass of red wine from the bartender and then stuffed a pretzel in her mouth while tapping her foot to the beat of the song.

The bartender delivered her wine. "Do you want me to open a tab?"

"No, I'm taking this to my room. You can give me the check now."

Once he delivered the bill, she scribbled her signature on it and then raised her glass. "Thanks."

As she left the bar, a group of people in front

of the elevator exploded in laughter. Suddenly self-conscious about her lack of underwear, her bare feet and the glass of wine in her hand, Scarlett pivoted toward the stairwell. She could handle three flights.

She slipped through the fire door and had started climbing the first set of stairs when the fire door behind her swung open. Looked like she couldn't avoid people even if she wanted to.

A whisper floated through the stairwell, and she slowed her steps. Had she stumbled upon another couple looking for a private spot for an intimate encounter?

The whisper turned into a lowered male voice. "We can't do it again, not with those two snooping around."

"I'll make it worth your while, just like last time."

The other speaker snorted softly. "Didn't work out that great twenty-five years ago."

Scarlett's muscles froze and she held her breath.

"Not my problem. I can take care of her, but you gotta get rid of him—and it all has to look like an accident."

"Shouldn't be too hard. He's got that gimpy leg and I heard he's kinda messed up in the head."

She backed up one step, the hand holding her wineglass, trembling.

The fire door above her burst open and Jim called down. "Hello?"

Terrified Jim would say her name, she spun around, taking the first step. Her toe hit the edge and she dropped her wineglass.

It shattered into a million pieces and broadcast her presence in the stairwell—loud and clear.

Chapter Fourteen

Jim jumped when he heard the crash of broken glass echo in the stairwell. Taking a step forward, he drew in a breath to call out to Scarlett. A split second later she appeared before him, her face white, a finger held to her lips.

Then he heard it. Heavy footsteps from the floors above.

Jim widened the door and grabbed Scarlett's arm when she reached him and pulled her into the lobby.

She gasped out one word: "Run."

If they were running from the people coming down those stairs, they wouldn't get very far. Jim pulled Scarlett in his wake as he careened down the hallway, looking for an out.

A supply room door stood open and Jim pushed Scarlett into the small room and yanked the door closed behind them. He braced his shoulder against the door in case it didn't lock and shoved his hand in his pocket and withdrew his Glock.

With his other arm, he held Scarlett against his chest where her heart pounded in rhythm with his.

His muscles coiled when the door to the stairwell crashed open, and Scarlett's body stiffened in his arms. He put his lips close to her ear, the damp tendrils of her hair tickling his nose. "Shh."

The carpet in the hallway muffled the footsteps heading their way, but to his ears they sounded like a herd of elephants.

He didn't know what the hell Scarlett had been running from, but the panic on her face told him everything he needed to know.

As the footsteps drew near, Jim licked his lips, his trigger finger tensing. The door handle went down and stopped with a click.

A bead of sweat traced Jim's hairline and dripped off his jaw.

Scarlett's warm breath permeated his T-shirt, but she didn't let out one sound.

The footsteps moved away, and Jim wedged his finger beneath Scarlett's chin and shook his head.

Would the men be waiting for them in the hallway? Did they know he and Scarlett had ducked into this closet? He pressed his ear against the door, barely discerning a murmur of voices. He and Scarlett would camp out in this little room all night if they had to—not the end to the evening he'd been anticipating.

With his back to the door, he slid to the floor, taking Scarlett with him. The maid's cart and the shelves stacked with towels gave him just enough room to sit with his knees bent.

He pulled Scarlett between his legs, and she rested her back against his chest, her head falling onto his shoulder. He kissed her temple and whispered, "Are you okay?"

She nodded.

He tightened his arms around her. He wanted the whole story, but he wanted to keep her safe more. They had time and he was patient. Hadn't he waited for his death in a filthy prison for nine months?

Over an hour later, Jim nudged Scarlett. "Are you sleeping?"

"Dozing. Can we talk now?"

"I think it's safe to leave our self-imposed captivity."

Twisting around, she placed her hands on either side of his face. "How are you doing? No flashbacks? No seizures?"

"Not even a twinge." Bracing one hand against the door, he rose to his feet and stretched as much as he could. He helped Scarlett up and rubbed her back.

"Just stay behind me while I open the door."

He pulled out his gun and leveled it in front of him.

"Do you think they could still be out there? Waiting? Watching?"

"I think they went out the side door, so maybe they think we ran outside. I haven't heard any noises on this end of the hallway, but keep yourself hidden behind me."

He pushed down on the door handle, holding his breath. Then he eased it open a crack and peered through it.

"I think we're good." He widened the door and stepped into the hallway, gripping his gun at his side. "We're taking the elevator. Just keep moving and run if I tell you to run."

He jabbed the elevator button to call the car and let out a breath when the doors opened immediately on the lobby floor. He urged Scarlett into the elevator ahead of him and crowded her into the corner until the doors closed.

For several more tense minutes, they rode the elevator to their floor and Jim didn't take another breath until he slammed the door to their room behind them.

Scarlett collapsed, throwing herself across the bed, one arm flung over her face.

He sat on the edge of the mattress and rubbed her foot. "What happened in the stairwell?"

She took a few more shaky breaths and hoisted

herself up on her elbows. "Two men are planning to get rid of us."

Jim hardened his jaw but didn't stop massaging Scarlett's cold, bare foot. "What men? Did you recognize them?"

"I couldn't see them. They were whispering and talking so softly, I couldn't distinguish their voices. The only reason I heard what they were saying was because of the acoustics in the stairwell."

"Why do they want to get rid of us? What else did they say?"

"Because we're meddling." She sat up and dug her fingers into his biceps. "They're planning more kidnappings."

"What?"

"They said something about repeating what they did twenty-five years ago. We have to tell Sheriff Musgrove. We have to warn everyone."

His hand moved up her leg and stroked her calf. "If they just put a target on your back, you're getting out of Timberline. Maybe I should've let them catch up to us so we could've identified them."

"They may know who I am, anyway." She fell back on the bed and hugged a pillow to her chest. "I dropped that glass of wine. They don't have to be rocket scientists to trace that back to the bar."

"Did you know the bartender?"

"No."

"So, if he tells them anything at all, he's going to say a woman with dark hair bought a glass of wine? Not a lot to go on."

"We don't have a lot to go on either, do we? Have you heard anything about Dax's condition?"

"I called the hospital when I was waiting for you to get your wine, and he's the same."

"Why did you come downstairs to find me?"

"You know, it's funny. I had a feeling something wasn't right, or maybe I wasn't happy with the idea of you wandering around on your own after everything that happened."

"Maybe I'm rubbing off on you. I'm the one with the ESP. How'd you even know I was in the stairwell?"

"I had just stepped off the elevator and saw you go through the door. There were a bunch of people waiting for the elevator, so I couldn't get your attention." His hand slipped up to her thigh. "And you're definitely rubbing off on me."

"I—I think one of the men was my uncle."

"How are we going to prove that? How are we going to prove anything?" He stretched out beside her. "Maybe it's time to call that FBI agent and tell him what we know."

"Which isn't a whole lot."

"Maybe he knows something that can make sense of what we've been grasping at. He's the one that made the connection between the Lords of Chaos and the drug trafficking."

"I'll call him tomorrow." She yawned. "This was supposed to be a relaxing getaway. I don't even have my glass of wine."

He trailed his hand up her body and slipped it beneath her T-shirt. He cupped one of her bare breasts in his hand, swiping the pad of his thumb across her peaked nipple. "I have ways of relaxing you that don't involve hot tubs or alcohol."

She sighed and her eyelashes fluttered. "We do have some unfinished business, don't we?"

"The thought of that unfinished business is the only thing that kept me sane in that supply closet." He rolled up her T-shirt and flicked his tongue inside her navel.

She combed her fingers through his hair. "Do you know what would relax me right now?"

Rolling his head to the side, he looked up at her through narrowed eyes. "Don't tell me watching TV."

She scooted out from beneath him and pushed him onto his back. Then she straddled him, yanked up his T-shirt and dragged her fingernails along his chest.

As she rocked against his erection, she whispered, "Forget TV. I have all the entertainment I need right at my fingertips."

He closed his eyes and let her entertain him.

SCARLETT KICKED THE tangled covers from her legs and rubbed her eyes. Through the closed bathroom door, she heard the shower running.

She scrambled from the bed. If Jim planned to boot her out of Timberline, she planned to get her fill of him first.

She crept into the bathroom, filled with citrus-scented steam, and whipped aside the shower curtain.

Jim grabbed her and pulled her under the stream of warm water.

She let out a yelp, and he laughed. "If you thought you could surprise an army ranger sniper, you've got another think coming, woman."

She kissed away a rivulet of water sliding down the flat planes of his chest. "Why did you sneak away?"

"Sneak?" He ran soapy hands down her back. "I got a call from the hospital about Dax and figured I'd better get ready."

"Is it bad news?" She dug her fingers into his sides.

"No. Not good news, either. He's still unconscious. They just called to tell me he's been moved to the main hospital."

"Are you going to visit him today?"

"Yeah. Like you said last night, he might be aware of what's going on around him." He kissed her. "I'll leave the shower to you."

She finished showering by herself, but it had

gotten a lot cooler without Jim…and a lot less interesting.

By the time she got out, he was dressed and looking at his phone with his eyebrows drawn over his nose.

"Is it Dax?"

He looked up. "A strange text from an unknown number."

"Really?" She tucked her towel around her body. Coming up behind him, she stood on her tiptoes and peered over his shoulder. "What's it say?"

Find the drugs, stop the kidnappings. Begin at the beginning.

"What?" She dropped to her heels. "Who sent that? What does it mean?"

He pulled out a chair and sat on the edge, tapping his phone against his chin. "Let's think about it for a minute. The Lords of Chaos were selling drugs back then. Even Gary Binder was involved at a low level and he was eliminated."

"And that drug trade had something to do with the kidnappings."

"The Lords had to be getting the drugs from somewhere because they weren't producers, and they had to be getting the money to buy the drugs from somewhere."

"Other criminal activities?" She massaged her temples. "How do the kidnappings fit in?"

Jim snapped his fingers. "Or the Lords paid in trade."

"What does that mean?"

"The Lords were doing something for the drug providers in exchange for product."

"Like what? Fixing their bikes?"

"Like kidnapping."

Scarlett clutched the towel around her waist. "Do you think the Lords of Chaos kidnapped those kids in exchange for the drugs?"

"Yeah, I do."

"A-and who supplied the drugs?"

"Think about it."

"My uncle."

"Bingo." Jim pressed the tip of his index finger in the middle of her forehead.

"But that would mean he ordered the kidnappings. Why? Why would Uncle Danny want to kidnap three children?"

"I don't know, but the conversation you heard in the stairwell last night indicates that he wants to do it again."

"Oh, no." She shook her head, the wet ends of her hair flicking droplets of water here and there. "This town can't go through something like that again. When Wyatt Carson kidnapped those kids, it just about tore Timberline apart at the seams."

"So, back to the text." He drummed his fingers on the credenza. "It sounds like there are some drugs missing."

"Once those drugs are found, they can be payoff for another round of kidnappings, but what's the purpose of the kidnappings? Where are those three—Kayla, Stevie and Heather?"

"I know you don't want to hear this, but I'm thinking it had to be some child-trafficking ring."

"My uncle?" She twisted the corner of her towel between two fingers. "I know he's not a good guy, but that?"

"What else? If some sicko was just murdering kids, he'd do it himself. Why go through some elaborate scheme of using drugs to compensate a bunch of bikers to kidnap the children?"

"And why those bikers?" Shivering, she crossed her arms.

Jim tucked her towel around her body. "Go get dressed and dry your hair. You're getting chilled."

"This conversation isn't helping." She turned and scurried back to the bathroom. "And I'm going with you to see Dax."

An hour later, after checking out via the TV, they slipped out of the hotel.

Scarlett watched the hotel entrance in her rearview mirror as she drove out of the parking lot. "If that was Danny in the stairwell, he can't know for sure that I was the one listening to him. I'm so glad you didn't call out my name."

"Me, too, but you need to watch your back."

"We both do." She tugged on the sleeve of his flannel shirt. "Do you think anyone's going to notice we're wearing the same clothes as yesterday?"

"I don't think it matters unless you want to go home and change."

"That's okay. I at least had a shower."

"I remember." He brushed one knuckle down her thigh.

"Jim, about last night…" She bit her bottom lip.

He squeezed her leg above her knee. "A night to remember."

Her nose tingled and she nodded. "I'll never forget it."

And maybe that's all she'd ever have of Jim Kennedy—the memories. Would they be enough?

SCARLETT PULLED INTO the parking lot of the main hospital, which was around the corner from the emergency entrance. Jim checked in at the reception desk on the ICU floor, and the nurse gave him Dax's room number and the go-ahead to visit him.

When Jim pushed open the door, he froze and Scarlett bumped into him.

Jim asked, "Who are you?"

Scarlett peered around Jim's large frame and met the heated gaze of a redhead sitting next to Dax's bed.

"Who the hell are you? If you take one more step into this room, I'm going to scream bloody murder for the nurse."

"Whoa." Jim held up one hand. "I'm Dax's brother, Jim Kennedy."

The redhead gave Jim the once-over and the deep lines around her mouth softened. "You're J.T. I see it now. You look just like my man—maybe a little softer around the edges."

"You're Belinda?"

"I drove here as soon as I got the call from that Deputy Stevens." She jerked her head toward Scarlett.

"Who are you?"

"I'm Scarlett Easton, a friend of Jim's."

"You're the one who found him." Belinda tossed her mane of hair over her shoulder. "I'm grateful to you."

Scarlett brushed past Jim and approached the bed. "How's he doing?"

"Not great, but he's a fighter. He'll pull through, but then he's got another problem."

Jim edged into the small room and took a spot at the foot of Dax's bed. "What would that be?"

"Didn't you get my text? If you don't find

those drugs and stop the kidnappers, they're going to come after Dax again—and this time they'll kill him."

Chapter Fifteen

Jim gripped the metal bar at the end of Dax's hospital bed. "You sent the text?"

"Dax told me to send it to you if anything happened to him." She flung her hand out toward Dax's still form. "Something happened to him."

Jim hunched forward, bracing his hands on the bed. "What do you know, Belinda? What did Dax tell you?"

She raised one eyebrow. "I'm not telling you anything here."

"Have you had breakfast yet?"

"A cup of coffee and a candy bar."

"Scarlett and I will buy you breakfast."

Pushing to her feet, she slung her leather jacket over one shoulder. "Dax said you were a hotshot sniper. You packing heat?"

Jim's hand moved to his pocket.

"Good, because I'm not going anywhere in this hick town without protection."

Scarlett put her hand on his arm. "Let's go to one of the restaurants in the new shopping center. Nobody needs to see us with Belinda at Sutter's."

"I like the way this girl thinks." Belinda shrugged into her jacket, covering the sleeve of tattoos that decorated her left arm.

Jim raised one finger and then leaned over his brother. "Hang in there, Dax. We're going to figure this out."

On their way to the elevator, Belinda stopped at the reception desk and rapped her knuckles on the surface as she hunched forward. "You're going to call me if there's any change, right?"

The nurse scooted her chair back an inch. "Yes, ma'am."

They stepped into the elevator, and Jim leaned toward Belinda, the smell of her heavy perfume tickling his nose. "Are they afraid of you?"

"They'd better be."

Belinda wanted to leave her car at the hospital, so Scarlett drove the three of them to the new shopping center, not far from the hotel where they'd stayed last night.

Jim swallowed. That hotel would always bring a smile to his face—wherever Scarlett wound up in the world. She only thought she wanted something more with him, but she was the same bright girl she'd been in high school and she'd made good on the promise of her youth.

He still had a long way to go, and she didn't need to be along for his journey.

"This place is open for breakfast." Scarlett pulled into a parking space and cut the engine. "Hopefully, we won't see anyone we know here."

"And if we do?" Belinda took the gum out of her mouth and stuck it in a wrapper.

"Why lie?" Jim shrugged. "You're Dax's girlfriend. You're here because he's injured and we're having breakfast with you."

Jim scanned the mostly empty restaurant and blew out a breath when he didn't recognize one person.

They settled in a booth in the corner, and the waitress poured them some coffee.

Jim planted his elbows on the table. "Tell us what you know, Belinda. If Dax had confided in me instead of you sending me cryptic messages *after* someone stabbed him, maybe he wouldn't be lying in that hospital bed right now."

"I don't know much." Belinda swirled some cream in her coffee. "Dax got out of the joint and came to me in Seattle. We had a good thing going. He was off the pills and the booze, and then he got a phone call that sent him over the edge."

"Dax? Nothing sends Dax over the edge."

"I know, right? This did."

Scarlett asked, "Did he tell you about the phone call?"

"He didn't say much. It had something to do with his past. He'd planned to ignore the whole thing until he found out you were in Timberline, J.T."

"Me? He went back to Timberline because of me?"

Belinda traced the rim of her coffee cup with the tip of her finger as she gazed into the caramel-colored liquid. "He was damned proud of you, J.T., of your service. He always bragged about his medaled-up little brother."

A knot formed in Jim's chest. "I didn't... We haven't had much contact."

Belinda lifted one narrow shoulder. "Dax is an ex-con. Just figured you didn't want him around."

Jim opened his mouth to ask a question and then snapped it shut when the waitress showed up. They ordered, and then Jim crossed his arms on the table, hunching forward.

"What did he think he was going to protect me from in Timberline?"

"He wouldn't tell me and he wouldn't let me come with him. All I know is the phone call had something to with whatever he'd been involved in here before with his old man. I got the feeling that the person on the other end of the line wanted him to pick up where the Lords had left off."

Scarlett tapped her water glass. "Rusty and

Chewy must've been called back, too, and it looks like Chewy's the only one who was game—unless he turns up dead like Rusty."

"What the hell is going on in this town?" Belinda cradled her coffee cup as if warming her hands. "Who's inviting the Lords back and for what purpose?"

Scarlett shot Jim a glance. "We're not sure and it's best you don't know anything more. What we think is that someone hired the Lords to kidnap children twenty-five years ago in exchange for a piece of the drug trade on the Washington peninsula."

Belinda's heavily lined eyes widened. "Dax kidnapping kids? I don't believe it."

"I'm not excusing him, Belinda, but he was just a teenager himself and influenced by our father. It was always hard to defy our old man. Dax was also using. Who knows what kind of pressure the Lords put on him."

"And the important thing?" Scarlett tapped Belinda's tattooed wrist. "He said no this time. That's why he's in that hospital bed fighting for his life."

The waitress brought their plates of food, but even after she left nobody started eating.

Belinda chased a potato around her plate with a fork. "I think Dax pretended to go along with it to buy time…and to protect you. I think he took a delivery of those drugs."

"I think you're right." Jim nodded and grabbed the ketchup bottle. "He took the drugs, hid them and then reneged on the deal."

"So, that's the text he had you send to Jim, Belinda, but what does it mean?"

"He didn't tell me. He texted me yesterday morning and asked me to send those words to his brother if anything happened to him. When I tried to call him to ask him what the hell was going on, he wouldn't respond." Belinda dabbed at her nose with a napkin.

"It has to mean something to me and to Dax— where it all started." Jim scratched the stubble on his chin. "Just wish he hadn't been so vague. Where what started? The whole Timberline Trio case?"

"Whatever happened to those kids?" Belinda finally sawed off an edge of her omelet and took a bite.

"Nobody knows. Poof." Scarlett flicked her fingers in the air. "They disappeared—no bodies, no trace."

Belinda's fork clattered against her plate where she dropped it. "That's horrible. I have a little boy and I can't even imagine. Dax is like a father to him. I still can't stomach the thought of him being involved in snatching children."

"And whoever was behind it twenty-five years ago wants to do it again. That's what I can't fathom. Why?" Scarlett shoved her full plate away.

Jim said, "As long as those drugs stay hidden, they're not going to get another chance. Whoever Danny has lined up to kidnap children this time is not going to do it without payment in the form of those drugs."

"Danny?" Belinda looked up from her coffee cup. "You *do* know?"

Scarlett kicked him under the table. "W-we have a good idea but no proof."

"Maybe that's where we start—with Danny. If he launched this whole plot years ago, maybe that's what Dax means. We need to start with him. We need to start at the reservation."

"Reservation?" Belinda's gaze darted between them. "This Danny, he's Native American like you?"

"Unfortunately, we're related, but forget everything we told you about his involvement. You did your part by sending that text to Jim. Now you just need to make sure Dax gets better." Scarlett aimed her fork at Belinda's plate. "And you can't do that on an empty stomach."

Jim dragged Scarlett's plate back in front of her. "And you can't investigate on an empty stomach."

"You're not sending me away?"

"How am I going to get on the reservation without you?"

"Granny has pretty much adopted you. I'm sure she'd be happy to entertain you."

Did she want to go back to San Francisco? He should be insisting instead of dragging her into this any further.

He tucked an errant strand of silky hair behind Scarlett's ear. "Then I'll go on my own."

"Oh, no." She jabbed a potato with her fork. "Granny might be ready to adopt you, but the rest of them still hate you. I'll be tagging along."

The three of them managed to finish their breakfasts and leave the restaurant without running into anyone they knew. The sooner Belinda could get Dax out of this town, the better.

When they dropped her off, Jim turned to Scarlett. "Can we go by the sheriff's station first? Stevens wanted me to check in today when Musgrove was there."

Their visit to the sheriff's station was a waste of time. The Timberline deputies didn't know much of anything about his brother's case, and Musgrove wasn't even at the station.

As they walked out, Jim mumbled, "How much golf can one guy play?"

"Especially at the tail of autumn on the Washington peninsula." Scarlett tipped her head back to take in the gray sky.

Jim joined her in the car and put his hand over hers. "One more stop? I'd like to drop by my place for a change of clothes."

"Of course." Her gaze flicked over her body. "Although you look fine to me."

"At least my boxers are dry."

As she started the car, her shoulders dropped and a smile touched her lips.

He'd never been much of a comedian, but someone had to lighten the mood. Scarlett had been so tense he was afraid she was ready to crack.

Hunching forward, he smacked the dashboard. "I think we're going to get to the bottom of this, Scarlett. Bit by bit, we're piecing things together."

She pulled onto the highway, back to the center of town. "Begin at the beginning. So, you think the beginning is with Danny and the reservation?"

"If he's the one who ordered the kidnappings or was part of the ring that originally ordered them twenty-five years ago, and it looks like he was. Unless…" Jim massaged the back of his neck as a shaft of pain shot through his skull.

She twisted her head to the side. "Unless what?"

"Maybe the beginning was with me. The kidnappings started after someone tried to snatch me, and instead of turning the guy in, my dad had a long talk with him. Maybe that's where it all started."

Scarlett's eyes got wide. "D-do you think your dad made some kind of deal with the kidnappers that night?"

"Maybe."

"Do you have any reason to suspect that it was Danny in your room that night?"

"I don't remember enough about him to make that call."

"I can see it for you."

"No."

"If a Quileute was involved, I'm sure I'll be able to sense that. The reason my vision worked so well with Beth St. Regis, that TV host, is because it turns out Beth was Quileute herself. It might tell us what we want to know, Jim."

"I think I already know it. I don't need further confirmation, especially at the risk of harming you."

Slicing her hand through the air, she said, "It doesn't harm me."

"It's not a bed of roses for you, either."

"Beds of roses are highly overrated. Look at you."

His brows shot up. "Me?"

"Your life hasn't been easy."

"That's an understatement. You don't think I wanted it otherwise?"

"Sometimes we don't get to choose. What you went through—all of it—made you the man you are today."

"A wreck?" His lips twisted.

"Jim Kennedy, you are the strongest man I've

ever met. Sure, you're battered, bloodied, beaten up—but not defeated."

"So, you're saying you're *glad* I went through hell?"

She smacked his arm. "Of course not. You know what I mean. I'm saying, if you can endure, I can endure. It's not a big deal."

"Let's see what your grandmother has to say first. If we spill everything we suspect, she might be able to fill in some details."

"But we won't find any drugs at the reservation. There's no way your brother could've hidden them there, and he wouldn't have wanted to."

"You're right about that." Jim drummed his fingers on his knee. "If the beginning was the attempt to kidnap me, maybe he hid them on our property."

"And maybe that's why he was stabbed. One of Danny's guys came looking for the drugs and Dax wouldn't tell him where they were."

When Scarlett pulled up to the cabin, the yellow police tape crisscrossed over the porch was a stark reminder of his brother's condition and the seriousness of their quest. Who would've guessed Dax Kennedy would turn out to be one of the good guys?

Jim opened the car door and turned to Scarlett. "Wait here. I'm going through the back and it'll take me two minutes to change."

"I hope you don't mind if I leave the engine running…just in case."

"You mean you'd leave me behind?"

"I mean in case someone approaches the house, so I can shift into gear and run him over."

"Oh, in that case." He flashed her a quick smile, but somehow he had the feeling she was dead serious.

It probably took him less than two minutes to exchange one pair of jeans and a T-shirt for another set and glance at the bloodstained entryway. If only Dax had confided in him. They could've handled this together. Dax still had the mind-set that he needed to protect his baby brother—just like he'd tried to protect him from their father during their childhood. Dax had played the role of the bad boy to allow Jim to be the good boy because the old man had needed—no, demanded—one son to follow in his criminal footsteps. Dax had sacrificed himself to spare him.

Jim swiped the back of his hand across his tingling nose.

He went out the back way and hopped in the running car. "You didn't see anything unusual?"

"No." She backed the car out of the driveway. "Unless you count stillness as unusual. The forest seems hushed today, like it's holding its breath."

"That's your hypersensitivity kicking in. Let's

just hope you're off base this time and there's no impending tragedy waiting for Timberline."

"If there is, we're on the path to divert it."

Scarlett drove to the reservation as if the answer was waiting for them there, but Jim didn't think it was going to be that easy.

He tapped her thigh. "Slow down, lead foot."

"I actually have my foot on the brake. It's speeding up downhill."

Scarlett waved to Prudence and her grandmother on the way into the reservation and then pulled up in front of Granny's house.

Scarlett called out as she opened the unlocked front door. Sitting in the same chair as before, Evelyn raised her head from her knitting, her dark eyes glowing in her lined face.

Scarlett crossed the room and dropped to her knees at her grandmother's side. "Are you okay, Granny? You look tired."

The old woman rested her hand on top of Scarlett's head as her gaze met Jim's. "Your brother was attacked."

"He was. The news spread already?"

"Is he going to live?"

"The doctors don't know yet. Fifty-fifty, they're telling me."

"Get him out of Timberline as soon as you can."

Scarlett touched Evelyn's knee. "What do you know, Granny? We think more kidnappings are planned, and there are drugs—missing drugs. As soon as those drugs get into the hands of the wrong people, the kidnappings will start."

Her knitting needles paused and she closed her eyes. "I don't know why he kidnapped those children."

"But you know who? Was it Uncle Danny?"

"Not then." Evelyn combed the yarn in her lap with trembling fingers. "Danny wasn't the leader, but he followed him and did his bidding as part of the Q-gang."

"Who, Evelyn? Who ordered the kidnappings and why?"

"Do you remember him, Scarlett? Rocky Whitecotton?"

A furrow formed between Scarlett's eyebrows. "Whitecotton? Tommy's family?"

"Yes, a cousin or something, a big man, a force in the tribe, but one that fomented dissent and hatred. He tried to recruit your father, but he had better luck with Danny."

"Are you saying Rocky Whitecotton was behind the kidnappings, Granny?"

"Everyone thought so."

"But nobody told the sheriff's department or the FBI?" Jim ground his teeth together. The Quileute were no better than the Lords of Chaos—protecting their own at the expense of others.

"We didn't know for sure, Jim. He terrified

the rest of us, threatened us. Nobody ever had any proof, just our suspicions."

Scarlett hopped to her feet, running a hand through her hair. "Rocky's been gone for years."

Evelyn nodded. "Just about twenty-five years."

"Why?" Scarlett flung her arms out to her sides like wings. "Why would Rocky Whitecotton kidnap three children from Timberline?"

"That I can't tell you, Scarlett. I can only give you the long-held suspicions of an old woman, but I know Rocky had some criminal organization going and he recruited Danny and tried to recruit your father."

A sharp pain lanced her temple and Scarlett sucked in a breath. "The accident that snatched away my family happened before the kidnappings."

"Yes." Granny's eyes dropped to the discarded knitting in her lap.

"Do you think…?" Scarlett took a turn around the room, the pain in her head turning into a dull throbbing. "Could my father have been punished for refusing to go along with Rocky?"

Granny placed a thin hand to her forehead. "You don't think that didn't occur to me all these years?"

Jim put his arm around her waist and drew her close. "And now Danny is back to do more of Rocky's bidding. I think it's time we call Agent Harper and tell him everything we know."

"But if Chewy or any of the other Lords get their hands on those drugs, they'll be ready and willing to carry out Danny's plans."

"We won't stop looking for the drugs, but we need the full resources of law enforcement to stop Danny, and there's no way we can count on Sheriff Musgrove."

Granny shook her head. "Danny may already have Musgrove in his back pocket. Don't trust him."

Her lips touched Jim's ear and she whispered, "Should we tell her about the clue?"

"Maybe she can help."

"Granny, Jim's brother left him a clue about the location of the drugs before he was attacked. It was, 'Find the drugs, stop the kidnappings. Begin at the beginning.' Does that mean anything to you?"

"If your brother knows about Rocky, it could mean here at the reservation, since Rocky seems to be the start of all of this, but Danny would know that, too."

Jim snapped his fingers. "Dax would leave me a clue that only the two of us would understand."

"Which brings us back to your father's cabin. That's where someone tried to kidnap you."

"Maybe Dax didn't mean the beginning of the Timberline Trio case or the Lords involvement in it. Dax had no way of knowing how much Scarlett and I had figured out."

Scarlett rubbed a circle on Jim's back. "The beginning of something between the two of you."

"We were never close, Dax and I. There was a big age gap between us, and he started following in Dad's footsteps pretty early on."

"So, it wouldn't be the beginning of the Lords of Chaos, since that wouldn't mean much to you."

Granny tapped her needles together. "The beginning—every birth is a beginning."

"We were even born in different hospitals."

"Even before that, then. The beginning for the two of you. The beginning of the Kennedy family. Something just the brothers would know."

Jim's body stiffened.

"You know? You remember something?"

"Dax was older than I was when our mom left. He always had a soft spot for her, never blamed her for leaving. He used to tell me that Mom said the only happy memory she had of our father was the day he proposed."

"The beginning." Scarlett squeezed his hand. "Was there someplace special he proposed?"

"Under the Kennedy Christmas tree."

"In the cabin?" Scarlett tilted her head.

"In the forest, by the old mine, where Carson stashed the kids he kidnapped a few months ago. My parents used to hang out at that mine—smoke cigarettes, do whatever teenagers do. There's a pine tree there and that's where my father proposed to her. For some reason, Dax loved that story, probably because it was the only softness in his life and reminded him of Mom."

"Do you think he'd bury the drugs there?"

"It's a place only he and I would know about."

"Then let's go. If we have some concrete proof in the form of drugs, the FBI is going to have to take a closer look."

"Let's go back to my place to get some shovels and tools. I'm going to call Duke Harper on the way."

Scarlett broke away from Jim and kissed Granny on the cheek. "Thanks for the information, Granny. Don't worry. We'll be okay."

Jim squeezed Granny's hands. "I'll take care of her, Evelyn."

When they got outside, Jim held out his hand. "Do you want me to drive?"

"I got this. I'm the one with the lead foot, remember?" She pulled away from Granny's house and made the right turn out of the reservation just as the skies opened and rain hit the windshield faster than the wipers could keep up.

The car crested the hill and started its descent, and Scarlett hunched forward in her seat to peer through the water sloshing across her windshield. The car picked up speed.

"I wasn't joking about the lead foot, Scarlett. Slow down."

"I—I can't." Scarlett pumped the brakes again

and heard the sickening sound of metal on metal as the car lurched to the right.

Her entire family had died in a car crash on this road, and it looked like she was about to meet the same fate.

Chapter Sixteen

Jim gripped the edge of his seat as the car skimmed the shoulder of the road, wet leaves and branches slapping his window. The greenery flew past him in a blur, and his heart thundered in his chest.

Scarlett had both hands on the steering wheel in a life-and-death struggle with the car, her knuckles white.

He shouted, "The parking brake. Put on the parking brake."

Scarlett stomped her left foot on the parking brake and the car shuddered and weaved. The back wheels fishtailed on the slick surface of the road and they started traveling sideways.

The car bucked and slowed down, but the tires were moving independently of anything Scarlett was doing with the steering wheel. The forest on the right side of the road was rushing at them as the car shook and coughed. A large tree trunk loomed out his window, and Jim yelled, "Step on the gas."

Scarlett didn't hesitate. The car jumped forward one last time before the back end hit the tree so hard his teeth rattled.

It heaved to a stop, and this time Jim didn't hesitate. "Open your door, Scarlett. We're getting out."

A tree was blocking his exit, so Jim clambered over the console almost into Scarlett's lap. The airbag hadn't deployed, which eased their escape from the car. Scarlett had opened the driver's-side door, and he pushed and prodded her ahead of him and out of the car.

He grabbed her hand and pulled her across the road just as the demolished car started emitting black puffs of smoke.

He parked Scarlett safely next to a tree on the other side of the burning car, shielding her body. He held his breath, waiting for an explosion.

Instead, the fire burned itself out on the metal of the car with the help of the pounding rain, leaving a smoking hulk at the side of the road.

Jim brushed a wisp of hair from Scarlett's wet cheek. "Are you okay? Your back? Your neck?"

She blinked. "I think so. You?"

"Rattled but not broken."

"Oh, my God." She covered her face with her hands. "Danny tried to do the same thing to us as he did to my family."

"He must've tampered with your car at the hospital or when it was at the reservation."

"He's serious, Jim. He wants to get rid of us so we'll stop meddling in his business."

"Once we find the drugs and get Harper involved, we can put a stop to this insanity. There's no way Chewy or any other Lord is going to do Danny's dirty work without getting paid in drugs first. Dax knew this."

A big rig loaded with lumber rumbled into view at the top of the hill. As the truck descended, the driver honked and slowed down. He yelled out his window. "You folks okay?"

"We're fine, but the car's totaled."

"Do you need me to make a phone call?"

Jim held up his cell. "I got it, thanks."

As the truck started moving, Jim called 911 to report the accident. Then he draped his jacket over Scarlett's head to protect her from the rain—at least he could protect her from that. She should've been back in San Francisco by now.

While he wrapped her in his arms, the familiar sound of sirens cut through the late-afternoon air. A squad car and a fire engine came over the hill, the fire truck pulling up behind Scarlett's car.

As soon as Deputy Unger got out of his car, Scarlett descended on him.

"Someone tampered with the brakes on my car. I'm almost sure of it, Cody."

The deputy scratched his chin. "You seem to be having a run of bad luck, that's for sure."

Scarlett choked. "A run of bad luck? Is that what you'd call it?"

"Are you accusing anyone, Scarlett? Do you know who's behind the attacks? Because if you do, we'd sure like to talk to him about Rusty Kelly's murder and the attempted murder of Dax Kennedy."

Jim shifted his weight to his other foot, just enough to touch Scarlett's shoulder. As much as Unger didn't respect his boss, Sheriff Musgrove was still his boss and Evelyn had just warned them against Musgrove. Jim would feel safer spilling his guts to a third party like Agent Harper.

"I—I don't know, but this," she said, and waved her arm at the smoldering car, "was no accident."

The firefighters had made short work of the flames licking at the underbrush around the car, and Jim watched as they put out any remaining live sparks on the car.

Unger gestured to Scarlett's car. "You're lucky that thing didn't blow."

"Jim got us out quickly, just in case." She put her hand through his arm.

The fire chief approached them, asked a few questions and confirmed that the car had been totaled—as if they didn't already know that.

"Did the inside of the car burn up? My purse is still in there, my cell phone. Can I get them?"

"Give it some time. There's still some hot metal on the car, and you don't want to get burned." The firefighters wrapped up and took off for an accident scene with injuries.

"What now?" Scarlett tapped the toe of her boot.

"The tow service is on its way, and we'll have an accident investigator from the county go over the car at the tow yard. If it's foul play, he'll spot it." Unger tucked his notepad into his front pocket. "Do you want me to wait for the tow truck driver with you?"

"How long is he going to be?" Jim peered at the setting sun. He had some digging to do.

"This rain wreaked havoc with more than a few motorists this afternoon. When I called in, the operator said he'd be out within the hour. I can give you two a ride."

Scarlett checked her watch. "We'll wait. I still want to get my purse and phone. Maybe the tow truck driver can help me get it."

"Suit yourself."

As Unger drove away, Jim dug his own phone out of his jacket pocket. "I'm calling Harper."

"Let me, and then I'll hand the phone over to you."

He dropped his cell into her open palm.

She tapped in the number and paused. Then

she shook her head. "Hello, Agent Harper, Duke. This is Scarlett Easton. Some new information has surfaced regarding the Timberline Trio case and the connection between the Lords of Chaos and…and certain members of the Quileute tribe. Can you give me a call when you get the chance?"

"Do you think he'll bite?"

"The FBI pulled Harper off the cold case just when he was starting to get somewhere. I think he'd like the chance to see it through."

She handed the phone back to him and he wrapped his fingers around her wrist and pulled her close. "Are you sure you're okay? We can take a trip to the emergency room."

"I'm going to be feeling the pain in my neck and back tomorrow, no doubt, but I'm not injured. Besides, we have someplace to be."

"Now that your car is out of commission." He jerked his thumb over his shoulder. "Do you think you can carry a couple of shovels while you're on the back of the bike?"

"I'm an expert biker bitch now." She pulled back her shoulders and tossed her head.

"If you say so." He rolled his eyes. "While we're waiting for this driver, I'm going to check up on Dax."

He called the hospital first and left a message with Dax's doctor. Then he called Belinda.

"How's Dax doing?"

"He's the same—no better but no worse. I had to set a couple of people here straight."

"What do you mean, Belinda?"

"Some nurse tried to kick me out of his room earlier, but I wouldn't budge. Came to find out that witch doesn't even work over here."

"What?" Jim tugged on the sleeve of Scarlett's jacket and set his phone to speaker. "What nurse?"

"Some little bitch who barged in here and told me Dax couldn't have any visitors right now."

"She wasn't an ICU nurse?"

"Nope."

"How'd you discover that?"

"When I wouldn't leave, she took off in a huff and I went to the nurses' station to complain about her. Those nurses told me it was still visiting hours and asked me about the nurse who told me to get out. I didn't get her name, but when I described her to them, she told me there was no ICU nurse like that."

Scarlett grabbed his arm. "Belinda, this is Scarlett. What did the nurse look like, the one who told you to get out?"

"Tall, black hair, big, pretty eyes, but cold as hell."

"Belinda, do not leave Dax's side, do you hear me?"

"Oh, I hear you, sister, and you don't have to tell me twice. I'm watching over him like a hawk."

When Jim ended the call, Scarlett kicked at the gravel on the shoulder of the road. "It's Tiana Gokey. It has to be. Danny is telling her to keep an eye on Dax. Who knows what else he's telling her?"

"My God. Would she go as far as killing him?"

"I don't know. I don't know what she owes Danny or thinks she owes him. This has to stop, Jim."

"As soon as we have some proof for Harper, it will." He spotted the tow truck and waved his arms in the air.

Forty minutes later, Scarlett had retrieved her belongings from the car and the charred vehicle was sitting on the flatbed of the tow truck.

"Can you give us a lift back to my place? It's on your way."

The driver nodded. "Sure, hop in."

They squeezed into the front seat next to the driver and he dropped them off at Jim's cabin.

As they collected a couple of shovels, a coil of rope and a pickax from the garage, Jim placed his hand on the small of Scarlett's back. "You don't have to go, Scarlett. I can do this by myself. I can tell you how it all turns out while you're having a glass of wine at a bar overlooking the city."

"I know you *can* do it by yourself, Jim." She turned toward him and cupped his chin with her hand. "But I want to be there with you. It's one of my people who caused this whole mess."

"Danny is no more your people than Slick is mine. We're not responsible for their actions. You don't have to put yourself in danger to prove anything or to redeem the Quileute."

"What danger? Nobody but us and Dax knows the location of those drugs, and we may be way off base."

"Don't downplay it. You've been targeted from the get-go."

"And that's why I need to see this through."

He handed her a shovel. "Then let's get busy."

He stuffed two flashlights and the rope in one saddlebag and tucked the head of the pickax in the other.

Once on the bike, Jim rested the two shovels across his lap and Scarlett grasped the handle of the pickax, holding it in place.

"Hang on with one arm. I'll go slowly. I had wanted to go out earlier while it was still light, but going under cover of the darkness might work out better."

As he started the bike, Scarlett's arm wound around his waist and he shoved off. They met only two cars on the way to the area of the forest that contained the abandoned mine where Wyatt Carson had stashed three children in an attempt to recreate the Timberline Trio case.

He cut the engine well before the entrance to the trail and rolled up silently. There were too many low-hanging branches for Jim to attempt to take his bike any farther into the woods, so he parked it off the road, concealing it behind some bushes. No need to advertise their presence here.

He handed Scarlett a flashlight and a shovel, and he took the other shovel and the pickax. He wound the rope around his body.

"Ready?"

She nodded, her eyes wide but her mouth determined.

They ducked into the woods, Jim leading the way with Scarlett close behind him. When they reached the clearing with the entrance to the mine and the tall pine where Slick had proposed to Wendy about a hundred years ago, Jim slowed and held out his hand.

He wanted to check the area first, but Scarlett charged past him. He made a futile grab for her jacket.

"If Dax just buried the drugs, there should be some signs of fresh dirt, even with the rainstorm coming through this afternoon. Hopefully, that rain made the ground soggy enough for some easy digging, and maybe Dax marked the spot somehow." Scarlett marched toward the pine, her flashlight sweeping the ground in front of her.

Jim choked out a harsh whisper as he staggered into the clearing after her. "Scarlett, hold on."

Then he heard it—the click of a gun's safety.

Scarlett yelped as Jim's flashlight illuminated

her pale face, an arm around her throat and a gun to her head.

Her uncle growled. "Drop the tools, Kennedy, and you might as well give up your gun right now."

"We called the sheriff's department, Danny." Scarlett squirmed in her captor's grasp. "They're on their way to meet us."

"Nice try, Scar, but I already know Granny warned you off Musgrove. You wouldn't have called him."

Chewy stepped from the shadows and waved his weapon at Jim. "Drop your stuff, Kennedy, and step toward the mine."

Jim hesitated only for a second before Danny placed the muzzle of his gun against Scarlett's temple. He tossed his shovel and the pickax in front of him, dug his gun out of his pocket and dropped it on the pile.

"How do you know what Granny told us? How did you know we'd be here?"

Jim licked his lips. Maybe if Scarlett could keep her uncle talking, he could get his weapon back. Chewy wasn't the brightest biker he knew.

"I had Jason bug her place."

Scarlett gasped.

"Don't worry about your little cuz. He didn't know he was doing it. He just thought he was delivering a gift to her from me—a sentimental gift that had belonged to my brother."

"Y-you killed my father, didn't you? Or Rocky had it done."

"Chewy, get Kennedy over by the mine."

"Move it, Kennedy." Chewy stepped forward, his gun gleaming in the low light, a shovel in his left hand.

Jim shuffled toward the mine entrance and glanced down. Someone had removed the boards from the top, leaving a gaping hole.

Chewy came at him, and Jim's muscles tensed, ready for the attack...or the bullet.

"Hate to do this to a Lord, but you were never one of us, were you?"

Chewy swung the shovel and hit him in the midsection, sending him into the dark abyss—again.

Chapter Seventeen

Scarlett screamed and broke away from Danny, but he grabbed her arm and yanked her back.

"Leave him, Scar. With any luck, he messed up his other leg. He's not your concern anymore. Your concern is finding those drugs."

Chewy rose to his feet from where he'd been crouching beside the mine entrance, aiming his flashlight into the depths. "J.T.'s at the bottom of the mine—probably dead."

Scarlett sobbed and then red, hot fury coursed through her veins and she clawed at Danny's face.

He smacked her cheek and she stumbled backward, catching a tree branch to stop her fall.

"Start digging. Once I get the drugs back and hand them over to Chewy and his guy, we'll be on our way. We'll go to another area, find other kids."

Chewy brushed his hair away from his small, dumb eyes. "But Rocky…?"

"Rocky doesn't have to know where the kids came from. He hasn't been in Timberline for years."

Scarlett touched her throbbing cheek. "What does Rocky Whitecotton want with these children? What did he do with them twenty-five years ago?"

"You don't need to know, Scar. Just start digging. I'll even let you live."

Scarlett snorted. She didn't believe that for a minute, but she had to hang on to the hope. If Danny and Chewy took the drugs and left her alive, she might be able to save Jim. She refused to believe he was dead. Refused to believe that fall had killed him.

She picked up a shovel, and Danny leveled his gun at her.

"Don't try anything stupid. Just start digging."

Chewy joined them and shined his flashlight at the ground under the tree.

A pattern of rocks emerged under the pine, and Danny must've spotted it the same time she did.

"There. Dax must've lined up those rocks like that. You should've warned me Dax's loyalties were with his brother, Chewy. I never would've handed the stash over to him."

"Prison must've changed him. He was always loyal to the Lords first."

Scarlett sniffed. Her guess was that Dax was

only loyal to the Lords so his younger brother wouldn't have to be. Had Jim realized that too before...? She squeezed her eyes shut. He couldn't be gone. She'd know. She'd feel it now if he were.

Danny poked his gun in her back. "Start digging, girl. You're going to do all the work, and we're going to make sure you do it."

Scarlett grabbed the shovel and drove it into the damp ground. She drew it out and tossed a shovelful of dirt to the side.

"That's not so hard, is it?"

After five minutes of digging, she wiped a drop of rain—or was it sweat—from her forehead. "Did you kill Gary Binder?"

"That loser didn't know much, but he knew enough to give that FBI agent some ideas. The agent was already looking into the Lords of Chaos. Gary could've given him the final link between the Quileute and the Lords."

"But why? Why did Rocky kidnap those children?"

Danny smacked the back of her head. "I told you. Don't worry about it. He gives his orders, and I follow them. If your father would've done the same, he'd be alive today and living the good life."

Tears burned behind Scarlett's eye and the dirt below her blurred. "And Rusty?"

"He wouldn't play along." Chewy cleared his

throat and spit. "Just like Dax. If Slick were alive, he would've been all in."

"Who tried to kidnap Jim?" She stomped her boot on the shovel to drive it into the ground again.

"That was me." Danny coughed. "I was no good at it, but I struck a deal with Slick Kennedy that night—the Lords would help us and we'd help the Lords."

"A match made in hell." She threw another mound of dirt at Danny's feet, hitting his silver-tipped boots.

"Why didn't you read Kennedy, Scar? That's what I was worried about with the two of you. He had the knowledge buried in his psyche and you had the ability to tap into it."

"We didn't need to go there. Granny knew your character. She knew you were involved, and then I heard your voice in the stairwell that night at the hotel."

"So, that *was* you." He kicked at the dirt. "But you never had any proof until Dax hid the drugs I gave him in good faith. One way or the other, we'll take care of him just like we did his brother."

Scarlett clenched her teeth. If Jim was really gone, she'd make sure there was no way in hell Danny ever got close to Dax. If he didn't kill her.

Her shovel hit something pliant but not as pliant as the mud she'd been shoveling. "There's something here."

"Keep digging." Chewy aimed his flashlight into the pit, highlighting the corner of a canvas bag.

Scarlett scraped her shovel across the top of it, revealing more of the canvas.

Danny shoved her aside. "Get that out, Chewy."

The big man hunched over the hole in the ground and grabbed the sack. He tugged and pulled until he freed it from its grave. Then he swung it onto the ground.

"This is it, Danny. Now I can have it all and I'll get you your kids. I'll get Rocky his new kids."

Danny swung his weapon from Scarlett to Chewy and shot him in the head.

Blood sprayed her cheek and she gagged as Chewy dropped to the ground, next to the drugs.

Danny laughed. "As if I'd trust that oaf to snatch some kids for Rocky. I guess it's back to the drawing board for me, but at least I have my incentive to get someone to do it."

Scarlett took a step back from the madness in her uncle's eyes. He'd never let her live and nobody would ever find Jim in time, even if he had survived the fall into the mine.

But she'd be damned if she'd die without a fight.

She had pivoted to face Danny, her fists raised, when a shot rang out.

For a split second she thought he'd shot her, but then she noticed the surprise on his face.

Danny's mouth dropped open as his chin hit his chest. Another bullet tore his torso and his head snapped back.

As he crumpled to the ground, Scarlett's gaze zeroed in on the entrance to the mine, where Jim's head was just visible over the edge.

Crying and laughing at the same time, Scarlett ran to him where he was dangling from a rope, a gun stinking of gun powder clutched in his right hand.

She dropped to the ground and flattened to her belly. Grabbing the rope tied under his arms and looped over a rock at the edge of the mine, she pulled him over the edge. With a grunt, she hoisted him up and over, and he collapsed beside her.

Smoothing a hand across his mud-caked cheek, she sighed. "You made it."

He grinned and pulled her down for a dirty kiss. "I've made it through worse and never has the reward been so great."

"WE CAN SEND you to a specialist in Seattle, Jim. I think that leg can be broken and reset." Dr. Harrison tapped his clipboard.

Jim shrugged and took Scarlett's hand. "It's just a limp. I don't mind if she doesn't."

"Me?" She leaned over and kissed his chin.

He'd never get tired of those lips.

"If you took away his limp, he might stop trying so hard."

"Give up? Never, not J.T." Dax beamed from his wheelchair, pride etched in every line of his face.

"It's an option. Just let me know if you're interested and I can make the recommendation." The doctor pointed at Dax. "And you—not too long in here. You need your rest."

Belinda curled her fingers around the handles of Dax's wheelchair. "Don't worry, Doc. I'll make sure he does everything he's supposed to."

Dax shrugged as she wheeled him out of the room. "I'll catch up with you later, J.T.—Jim."

Jim held up a clenched fist. "Proud of you, bro."

When Dr. Harris followed Belinda and Dax out of the room, Scarlett rested her head on his chest.

He'd never get tired of that, either.

"Will it be hard for Dax to leave the Lords? It was hard for you."

"Different time. The Lords are pretty much done in this area. Nobody's going to be coming after Dax."

"I still can't believe you made it out of that mine and were able to get to the gun strapped to your leg."

"Chewy didn't check me for any more weapons. Snipers always carry a spare. And I had that rope wrapped across my body. I guess he missed that, too."

"Or maybe he figured the fall would incapacitate or kill you."

"He figured wrong." He traced a line from her earlobe along her jaw. "Agent Harper dropped by. Did you see him?"

"No. He was here earlier?"

"The FBI was able to trace the drugs to Danny, but they still don't have any idea where Rocky Whitecotton is. It's like he fell off the face of the earth twenty-five years ago."

"So, the FBI doesn't know why he wanted those children and what he did with them?"

"The Timberline Trio is still a mystery. If they can't find Whitecotton, maybe we'll never know what happened to those kids and why."

"I feel for those families, but I'm done. I'm done with Timberline for a while, except for Granny."

"Did you tell Jason what he'd done?"

"He feels bad. He figured Danny was up to no good, but he needed the money he was offering."

"I'm sure he wouldn't have done it if he thought it was going to put you in danger."

"That's his problem." She tapped her head. "He doesn't think."

"And you? What do you think?"

"About what?" She wedged her chin on his chest and gazed into his eyes.

"Seattle."

"I've always liked Seattle."

"There's a training program for counselors there that sounds good. I can even start working at the VA center right away."

"That would be great for you, Jim."

"And maybe for you? I talked to the VA about that art therapy. The folks there are interested… if you are."

"Us? Working together?"

"I think we make a good team—that is if you're willing to throw in with a battered and bruised vet."

"Battered and bruised, but not broken."

She pressed her lips against his and he smiled beneath her kiss. Not broken, not broken at all.

* * * * *

Carol Ericson's miniseries
TARGET: TIMBERLINE *comes to a
gripping conclusion next month when*
IN THE ARMS OF THE ENEMY *goes on sale.*

*You'll find it wherever
Harlequin Intrigue books are sold!*

LARGER-PRINT BOOKS!

HARLEQUIN

Presents®

GET 2 FREE LARGER-PRINT
NOVELS PLUS 2 FREE GIFTS!

PASSION
GUARANTEED
SEDUCTION

YES! Please send me 2 FREE LARGER-PRINT Harlequin Presents® novels and my 2 FREE gifts (gifts are worth about $10). After receiving them, if I don't wish to receive any more books, I can return the shipping statement marked "cancel." If I don't cancel, I will receive 6 brand-new novels every month and be billed just $5.30 per book in the U.S. or $5.74 per book in Canada. That's a saving of at least 12% off the cover price! It's quite a bargain! Shipping and handling is just 50¢ per book in the U.S. and 75¢ per book in Canada.* I understand that accepting the 2 free books and gifts places me under no obligation to buy anything. I can always return a shipment and cancel at any time. Even if I never buy another book, the two free books and gifts are mine to keep forever.

176/376 HDN GHVY

Name _____ (PLEASE PRINT) _____

Address _____ Apt. # _____

City _____ State/Prov. _____ Zip/Postal Code _____

Signature (if under 18, a parent or guardian must sign)

Mail to the **Reader Service:**
IN U.S.A.: P.O. Box 1867, Buffalo, NY 14240-1867
IN CANADA: P.O. Box 609, Fort Erie, Ontario L2A 5X3

**Are you a subscriber to Harlequin Presents® books
and want to receive the larger-print edition?
Call 1-800-873-8635 today or visit us at www.ReaderService.com.**

* Terms and prices subject to change without notice. Prices do not include applicable taxes. Sales tax applicable in N.Y. Canadian residents will be charged applicable taxes. Offer not valid in Québec. This offer is limited to one order per household. Not valid for current subscribers to Harlequin Presents Larger-Print books. All orders subject to credit approval. Credit or debit balances in a customer's account(s) may be offset by any other outstanding balance owed by or to the customer. Please allow 4 to 6 weeks for delivery. Offer available while quantities last.

Your Privacy—The Reader Service is committed to protecting your privacy. Our Privacy Policy is available online at www.ReaderService.com or upon request from the Reader Service.

We make a portion of our mailing list available to reputable third parties that offer products we believe may interest you. If you prefer that we not exchange your name with third parties, or if you wish to clarify or modify your communication preferences, please visit us at www.ReaderService.com/consumerchoice or write to us at Reader Service Preference Service, P.O. Box 9062, Buffalo, NY 14240-9062. Include your complete name and address.

HPLP15

LARGER-PRINT BOOKS!
GET 2 FREE LARGER-PRINT NOVELS PLUS
2 FREE GIFTS!

HARLEQUIN®

Romance

From the Heart, For the Heart

YES! Please send me 2 FREE LARGER-PRINT Harlequin® Romance novels and my 2 FREE gifts (gifts are worth about $10). After receiving them, if I don't wish to receive any more books, I can return the shipping statement marked "cancel." If I don't cancel, I will receive 4 brand-new novels every month and be billed just $5.09 per book in the U.S. or $5.49 per book in Canada. That's a savings of at least 15% off the cover price! It's quite a bargain! Shipping and handling is just 50¢ per book in the U.S. and 75¢ per book in Canada.* I understand that accepting the 2 free books and gifts places me under no obligation to buy anything. I can always return a shipment and cancel at any time. Even if I never buy another book, the two free books and gifts are mine to keep forever.

119/319 HDN GHWC

Name	(PLEASE PRINT)

Address	Apt. #

City	State/Prov.	Zip/Postal Code

Signature (if under 18, a parent or guardian must sign)

Mail to the **Reader Service:**
IN U.S.A.: P.O. Box 1867, Buffalo, NY 14240-1867
IN CANADA: P.O. Box 609, Fort Erie, Ontario L2A 5X3

Want to try two free books from another line?
Call 1-800-873-8635 or visit www.ReaderService.com.

* Terms and prices subject to change without notice. Prices do not include applicable taxes. Sales tax applicable in N.Y. Canadian residents will be charged applicable taxes. Offer not valid in Quebec. This offer is limited to one order per household. Not valid for current subscribers to Harlequin Romance Larger-Print books. All orders subject to credit approval. Credit or debit balances in a customer's account(s) may be offset by any other outstanding balance owed by or to the customer. Please allow 4 to 6 weeks for delivery. Offer available while quantities last.

Your Privacy—The Reader Service is committed to protecting your privacy. Our Privacy Policy is available online at www.ReaderService.com or upon request from the Reader Service.

We make a portion of our mailing list available to reputable third parties that offer products we believe may interest you. If you prefer that we not exchange your name with third parties, or if you wish to clarify or modify your communication preferences, please visit us at www.ReaderService.com/consumerchoice or write to us at Reader Service Preference Service, P.O. Box 9062, Buffalo, NY 14240-9062. Include your complete name and address.

HRLP15